Sweet Beginnings

LOVE HAPPENS • BOOK TWO

SUSAN WARNER

Sweet Beginnings

One

She was standing on a ten-foot ladder in a skirt with a shoebox hanging around her neck, with a bird inside.

"I can feel you hopping away in the box. When I get you next to the branch, you better hop on. I've got guests coming, and I don't need them to see little birdies who don't know how to stay in their nests."

Hannah Jenkins was cautiously making her way up the ladder, which leaned precariously against the house. This was just her luck. Today she was waiting for her first guests to come to her home. She needed some extra income and had decided this would be the way. If the city could make money on Airbnb, she could too.

It was all going well; she had picked out the perfect outfit for her brand-new guests. They were from New York, so she made sure she had on a skirt and blouse to look country chic. Then she heard it—the chirping of a baby bird. Hannah looked at the bird, and she was ashamed to say she thought about ignoring it. Then a vision of one of the cats prowling around the property came to mind. Hastily looking down the driveway, she started to think.

Looking up at the large tree next to the house, she saw the bird's nest in the "V" of the two branches that touched the side of the house. Did she have time? She needed this BnB thing to work. Trying to support a teen in a town without a lot of opportunities and an ex who had to be reminded to send support was hard. Then it happened again! The little bird chirped.

Hannah hurried to the side of the house to grab the compacted ladder. It took her twice as long to move it, as she was trying to make sure her skirt didn't get smudged. She knew she should have worn the dark skirt, but no, she wanted to look all delicate and floral. Hannah didn't have enough words to go over how ill-planned this was. She extended the ladder against the house and then reached for the bird, which promptly hopped away.

"You've got to be kidding me. I'm trying to help you!" Hannah exclaimed. Looking around, she saw a shoebox in the recycling, popped a hole in the top and through the bottom with her finger, threaded some recycling twine, and made a circle. She scooped the bird into the box, hung it about her neck, and then up the ladder she went. The bird hopped and chirped. "I know, little guy, almost there."

As if on cue, the adult birds returned, and none looked happy to see her coming toward the nest.

"I want you to know this is not a daily service," Hannah said, as she stood on the last rung of the ladder. She took the box from around her neck, opened the box, and the chick happily hopped back to the nest. That was when she heard wheels on gravel. She looked over her shoulder and just what she was trying to avoid was coming to pass. Her new guests were arriving, and she was on the ladder. Hoping to minimize the moment, she began to descend the ladder. An errant wind blew, ruffling her skirt. Hannah instinctively grabbed for her skirt to hold it down, and at the same time shook the ladder.

"I'm coming, don't move," someone called from below. "I'll steady it for you."

Hannah shook her head, trying to sort through all the acceptable answers as to why she would be on the ladder. "No worries, I've got it," she called out. "My timing is always off," she muttered to herself.

Hannah looked down and saw a man at the bottom of the ladder, and all she could think of was to hold the skirt tighter as she moved down. "Please step away from the ladder. I'm fine," she called out.

"It's no problem. I'm here," the man persisted.

"No, really, you should move away."

Hannah had slowed her descent as she realized the man wasn't moving. She was about to call out to the man, telling him to move aside so she could finish her descent without him knowing what color her underwear was, when another wind came. Then, like a perfect storm, it happened. Hannah bent down to gather more of her skirt. The ladder held firm, and her grip wasn't as tight as she thought. The next moment, though, the only thing she had in her grasp was her skirt.

It wasn't a far fall. It was even less of a fall because she never hit the ground. Instead, she fell into the firm grasp of the stranger who didn't know how to take basic instructions.

Hannah was cradled in the arms of what she could only deduce was one of her new renters. She released her skirt, tapped him on the arm, and he set her on her feet. As he put her on her feet, she couldn't help but notice the five foot eleven inches of him, giving him the perfect height to look into her eyes. Or how his arms didn't shake when she was in his arms, and at one hundred eighty pounds or the publicly disclosed one hundred and sixty, she wasn't a lightweight. When she braced her hand against his chest before he set her down, she didn't feel his heart thumping. She was thrilled. Injured people didn't make long staying guests.

"Excuse me. Are you okay?" she asked, smoothing her skirt down. She stood up to her full five feet eight inches and extended her hand. "Welcome to the Pearl B and—"

Hannah scrunched up her face and did a double take. This wasn't just any city renter. His face had been all over the tabloids not even six months ago. In the small town of Sweet Blooms, when one of our own hits the news, it was news for four months past the time it was news for everyone else. According to the town gossip, he was the spitting image of his father. The married women still spoke of how the Cade men had all been gifted with looks. They could have been models if it weren't for the fact, they all worked with their hands. He had the Cade trim beard, with the long eyelashes that would give the fake lashes a run for their money. Each one of their boys was named for someone in the Bible. It was said they needed it to balance out their sinfully good looks.

Adam Cade, Fortune 500 owner, and the man who walked away from the beautiful cover model Nadia Larson. The rumors ran rampant; what would make a man walk away from the most beautiful woman on the earth?

They had been photographed together, and he went from being an up and coming entrepreneur who was modernizing his family business and making the top 250 companies to watch, to being the man who would make perfect children with the perfect woman. Nadia Larson was the top model on both hemispheres. Adam brought a down-home quality that never went out of style. He didn't work out at the gym; he worked with his hands making furniture as his father had before him. If there was a picture of a country wholesome good guy, it would be Adam Cade.

Adam didn't forget his roots. He came to Sweet Blooms to bring business to the smaller ones in town. He always referred to his friends and business acquaintances to meet at Sweet Blooms. More importantly, when a natural disaster struck Sweet Blooms, he came and helped rebuild houses and invested money. They had never met before. No one wanted to speak to Henry Jenkins, and the woman who had been fool enough to marry him wasn't held in that high regard either. Adam Cade was the town hero, and he was here. She had just been caught by him.

It was a bit much. All her original insecurities started to flood back. This BnB thing had been a last resort. What if they didn't like her house? What if they didn't like the two rooms? This was Adam Cade; he had stayed in the best of the best, and he was coming to stay in her home for a week. What had she been thinking when she thought up this plan?

He smiled at her and held out his hand. "Thank you."

"For?" she asked, confused.

"I've never been able to introduce myself, as I'm the man who just saved you."

Hannah was transfixed watching his mouth move. She wasn't really into the bearded look, but she had to admit it looked good on him. Then his words penetrated the fog of male appreciation.

"Really? Well, you still can't."

His smile grew, and a perfect mouth was revealed. "I don't know. I seem to remember it a little different," he said, looking at her.

Hannah cocked her head to the side and folded her arms over her chest. "Let me tell you what really happened. I was coming down the ladder just fine when a man stood impolitely at the bottom of it and would not acknowledge common decency and move. Instead, he loitered at the bottom of the ladder, stopping me from getting down in a timely manner before the wind came."

"Ouch! I think I prefer my version better. Saving the helpless damsel in distress before she fell to her—"

"I wouldn't have needed saving if you had just moved! Now let's not squabble over the truth. You're here. Let's get you settled. How many bags do you have?"

He didn't move; he just stared at her, and for a moment she thought he had a sparkle from his white teeth. Okay, it was definitely time to move this along. She didn't have time for men. Besides, she had a talent for picking all the worst ones out of the bunch. So, Adam Cade may look like a shiny apple, but she knew there was something about him that was rotten to the core.

He held his hand out behind him. "I'll bring in the luggage. Let me introduce my grandmother, Delilah Cade."

"Welcome, Mrs. Cade," Hannah said, trying not to stare at the woman. You could tell she was older, but the Cade gene of good looks wasn't just on the male side. Hannah's mother had often cautioned her that she could never hide her thoughts.

Delilah Cade smiled and grabbed Adam's hand. She was the epitome of classic beauty and grace.

"I know my grandson means the best," Delilah said. "Forgive him. He's a do first and sort it out later kind of guy."

"It's no problem, gran," Adam said. "I'm sure Ms. Jenkins was glad I was here to assist."

Hannah had to clench her teeth to let the moment of frustration pass by. She warred with telling him what she really thought and not having to break the news to Delilah Cade, who looked at her grandson with such love and devotion, not even she had the heart to let her know the truth.

"I'm sure Mr. Cade had the best of intentions. However, I really will have to ask that he try to control his take charge inclinations. Things are a little different out here, and I want to make sure he stays safe."

Adam laughed. "I have to say that this is a first for me. I think you're trying to put me in my place."

Hannah smiled at him. "All of us mortals have this experience. I'm sure you, too, will adjust."

"Thank you for the lesson, Hannah. Not many people disagree with me when I'm right."

"Right?" She took a deep breath.

"Why don't we move on. Follow me, and I'll show you to your rooms."

She slowed her pace to make sure Mrs. Cade wasn't rushed. She was so conscious of the warm, deep tones of his voice as he spoke to his grandmother. She could see his shadow in front of her. Was everything about him impressive? She really needed to focus.

She knew she had a rotten apple to the core pick-a-man syndrome. If she was looking for someone, and she wasn't, but if she were, it wouldn't be with super famous Adam Cade. She would like someone who had some very specific characteristics. He would have to be happy with her baby, Nathan, who wasn't really a baby anymore. He was about to become a teen without a dad. She would also be looking for someone who would be happy with her. Is Adam Cade happy with her? That was a non-starter. A man didn't rebound from the most beautiful woman in the world to be with plain jane and her son. Adam would find his new Nadia because Barbie always found Ken.

Hannah had learned a lot about herself since her split with Henry. She knew that she could depend on herself to provide for herself and her son. She knew she was strong, determined, and had a quick mind. She also knew her hobby of making quilts and blankets was a budding business that would provide for her and her son. She was self-sufficient. She also knew the town of Sweet Blooms had some small-minded people. While most of the residents were understanding, there were some who didn't think the divorced wife of Henry Jenkins should be living on the Jenkins farm. It didn't matter to them that Henry hated it. She had been judged a golddigger who had stolen Henry's land in the divorce. As an owner of one of the original tracts of land in Sweet Blooms, she was grandfathered to the council, but that hadn't endeared her to anyone either.

She had spent a lot of time trying to get accepted by the town. Not for her sake, but for Nathan's. He was going to go to high school next year, and he had enough problems without being reminded his mother was an outsider and, by default, so was he.

"Ms. Jenkins?"

"Yes?" she snapped.

Hannah had been so far in her thoughts she had walked them to their room and was standing in the doorway. "I see these are two adjoining rooms and the bathrooms are inside like the brochure says. Is there anything else you wanted to show us or house rules?"

She shook her head wildly. "No, no. I'm so sorry."

"It's no problem. You've had a harrowing day." Adam grinned at her and leaned against the door in front of her. "I'll see you tonight?"

Tonight? she repeated to herself. *That's right!* Mr. rotten somewhere at his core was living here for the week. She would provide room, board, and two meals a day—breakfast and dinner. "Of course, I'll see you later."

She heard Delilah call out, "I'll see you later, dear."

"Of course, I'll see you later," Hannah replied.

She stepped away from the door without acknowledging Adam anymore. When the door was closed, Hannah looked to the heavens and couldn't believe the way she had acted. She had to get dinner together. Maybe having a different focus would help her not focus on Adam Cade.

Cooking was dependable, she thought. It was a set of clear instructions held together by order and then executed in such a way that practically guaranteed a satisfying result. But men—they didn't seem to comprehend the word dependable. Looking at the way Adam had left Nadia, dependable might be a foreign word for him too. For a moment, when she came down from the ladder, and she was in his arms, she felt safe and treasured.

It wasn't the chemistry that couples are built on. It was the hint of something that could be. Almost a taste of what might be. Even Hannah had to admit it felt good. The bad news was it was happening with her guest. Her guest had dumped the most beautiful woman in the world. He was so way out of her league.

In Adam's world of perfection, she didn't even exist. She would never be given a second look because she was honest enough to know she was attractive, but she didn't stop men in their tracks. The real problem she found was she was too trusting, and she believed in love. Believed in putting in the work through sickness and health.

Shaking off her maudlin thoughts and concentrating on dinner, she was able to bring her mode back up. Fashion came and went; maybe a good woman who wanted to stand by a man and support him would come back in style too. Until Mr. Ordinary showed up, she'd better make sure she was self-sufficient and could take care of her son.

Adam had put away the luggage and had taken a walk around the house. It was a five-bedroom home that seemed like it would be more suited for a large family than a bed and breakfast. The floors had been recently waxed, and the railing on the staircase was shining.

However, other little things told him all was not as new as she wanted it to be. If he looked hard enough, he could see her attempts to hide what he thought was damage to the house. The connecting door between the rooms at first glance looked like it was there for guest convenience, but he could see how the paint was a little darker around the door than the rest of the room. The blue was a good color to use, but he could still see the signs of water damage. If he had to guess he'd say that the door was installed as a way to hide some leaking pipes, and Ms. Jenkins hadn't been able to quite find a perfectly matching blue paint.

As he walked through the house, the builder in him could see it had great bones. This was a house he could happily spend some time renovating.

On the side of the house was a garden that had been fenced off and a small, cushioned bench sat inside the perimeter. That was where he was going to take his grandmother. He'd been thinking about his life since the breakup with Nadia, and he needed a change. An idea had been forming in his head for that change and he'd recently formed a plan to start a new career in Sweet Blooms. He had carefully thought over his plan to start a new venture in Sweet Blooms and he looked at others who had done the same thing.

Now that the time was at hand and he could see his grandmother coming around the corner, he was nervous. Grandma Delilah was a spitfire to be sure. She was also the most level-headed person he knew and the one person whose opinion mattered to him more than anything. She was also the one person who supported him no matter what.

When Adam's father found out he wanted to join the family business, he had told Adam no. Daniel Cade said he wanted better for his son than to be a laborer. His grandmother had recognized his talent and got him into an apprenticeship.

When his father passed away, his grandmother had been his rock. When his sister and brother thought it was better to sell the struggling company, his grandmother had stood by him to keep it and make it grow. Now, Designs by Cade was known throughout America and they had so many requests in the pipeline that they had to turn business away.

He had done his duty by his family and made sure they were provided for and happy in their business. He had groomed his sister Corinne to take over because she was good at taking charge on a higher level. His brother Luke didn't thrive in the office. He enjoyed doing the designs and couldn't stand being in meetings every day so Adam left him alone to his designs.

Now Adam was ready to do something for himself.

The last fiasco with Nadia had brought it to bear that it was time for him to live his life. The rumors about their breakup got more fantastic as time went on. In truth, Nadia broke up with him. She wanted it to leak that he had left her because she needed some sympathy to boost her career. Nadia was a lovely woman, but he wanted one that would just be happy being with him. Nadia was happy as long as he wanted to be in the limelight with her.

He always enjoyed coming back to Sweet Blooms. Over the years he had made friends here and helped people. Some of those people had even come to call him Delilah's Boy. He couldn't think of a reason gran would say this wasn't a good idea, but until it was done, it was still up in the air.

"I've been waiting on you, gran," he said, holding out his hand to her. When she put her hand in his, it felt so warm. It was just one more sign of how nervous he was. In the end, he'd do what the best thing for him was, but if she didn't agree, he'd be less for it. His gran had been the one to always support him through thick and thin.

"I see something is weighing on you," she said.

"I was glad when you wanted to come here to get away for your birthday. It's like it was a sign," he started.

"Hmm, go on." She eyed him knowingly.

"I've decided that I want to step down from the company. I want to start to live a normal life. The company is set up so Corinne can run it. Luke will still do designs. They don't need me there anymore, and I need to move on." He said it in one breath, and suddenly, the load was off his chest.

"If you made up your mind, why are we out here?"

Adam laughed. "Because I wanted to know your thoughts. Having two made-up minds is better than one."

She shifted on the bench. "All the cushions in the world won't make this bench comfortable. You should give her some dead stock on the old treated pieces."

Adam smiled. Gran could throw a curve ball at you while she thought on things.

"Well, I have some questions."

"I thought you would."

"Did you decide you wanted to walk away because you're running from Nadia?"

"Ouch, gran! I'm not running. I will say the whole event helped me to see what I really wanted, and how it wouldn't really be possible on the road I was on."

His grandmother turned to him and pulled him into her arms.

"I'm so glad you're looking out for you because I was starting to worry," she said. "You know I'm beyond proud of you. Besides that, I'm not getting any younger, and I'd like to see some of my great-grandchildren."

"I don't even have a wife, and you're looking for grandchildren."

"Goals, boy, you have to set goals," she laughed. "When and where would you be making this great exodus?"

"I wanted to move here to Sweet Blooms."

Delilah laughed out loud and patted her chest to catch a breath. "You do know that all the women in this town will be flocking to you in no time."

"I'm not going to tell everyone. I'm going to take my time and not make any public announcements, to avoid the publicity."

Delilah patted him on the leg. "Boy, you may know the city, but you don't know small towns. If you stay here long enough, you'll find that people find out what's going on almost as quickly as you think it."

"Ah-hem, I'm sorry to interrupt, but dinner is ready if you are?" A soft voice said behind them.

Adam and Delilah turned to see Hannah at the gate. Delilah smiled at Adam. He wanted to ask her what the smile was for, but she brushed him off and said she had to get to supper, or they'd offend Hannah.

Later that evening, Hannah went out to her garden—trying to find some peace from the day—when her cell phone rang. Five minutes later, she regretted not ignoring the phone.

"You have got to be kidding me," Hannah said on her cell. Shaking her head in disbelief, she walked out the back door and into the garden. She grabbed her pink foam knee pad and shook the loose dirt from it. She could tell she'd need a relaxing distraction in order to get through this phone call. She picked up a pitcher and dropped water over her garden tools to make sure they were clean.

"Hannah, I am dying! I need to stay in the hospital for a little longer," the voice on the other end of her headphone whined. Hannah grabbed the shovel, rinsed it, and then put it back in her kit.

"We're all dying, Henry. Your son is waiting here for you to come this week. You promised!"

"The hospital won't let me out."

"Okay, which hospital are you in?" Hannah was so tired of his excuses. The only thing she could focus on was how Nathan was going to be disappointed again.

"Well, I wouldn't want to put anyone out. It's no place to see a man in." Henry stammered and backpedaled as he tried to bolster his thin excuse.

"Tell me, Henry, what new opportunity is going on?" She bit out each word, trying not to let the bitterness or the held back tears, seep into her voice.

"The city is a great place, Hannah. You always think it's the city that's coming between us. I can't help it if the city has these great work opportunities for me. I don't understand why you stay in Sweet Blooms anyway. There's nothing here for you. All the opportunity for you can be found in the city. Think about what the income could do for you and Nathan."

She wouldn't argue with Henry about how great he thought the city was. When it came to choices, the city always won. It was more important than her, and it was more important than their son Nathan.

Exhausted with it all, she sat back on her haunches and looked at her faded denim jeans.

"Henry, are you coming, yes or no?"

"No, I can't. I told you—"

"Fine, when are you going to tell Nathan?"

"Well, I don't know when the hospital will let me on the phone again. So maybe it would be best if you told Nathan. I-I mean, I'll try, but just in case, make sure you tell him."

"Henry! No, I—"

"Hey, I gotta go. Thanks, Hannah."

The next moment she was listening to the dial tone. She dropped the cell in her pocket and tried not to imagine how her son would take the news when he returned home in a couple of days.

Two

Hannah was ready to go out and do the morning chores. She had two more days before Nathan came back home from visiting with his Aunt Sally in town. She would be able to get the gardening done in order to save a little on her grocery bill. Besides that, work in the garden was more of a relaxation moment for her.

She picked up her gardening bag at the door, along with her hand tools and her knee pad to lean on. When she opened the door, the morning breeze greeted her. She took a deep breath and walked around the house to the garden. She loved this time of day. The birds were up. The sky was blue, and she could think her thoughts alone. She didn't let worries crowd in on this time—it was her time.

As she rounded the corner, standing at the gate to the garden was Adam. He waved at her and smiled.

"You going to be doing some gardening?" he asked with that perfect smile and deep voice. "Maybe I can give you a hand?"

The first words that came to her mind were *no you cannot give me a hand, this is my private time before my son gets back, leave.* However, she held her tongue because she remembered what she had heard coming around the corner. Adam Cade was looking to not only stay in Sweet Blooms, but he was also looking to settle down. She didn't want to make an enemy of yet another resident of Sweet Blooms.

She looked at him standing there, holding the garden gate opened for her. He had on black jeans and a blue and black plaid shirt. She wondered if his whole wardrobe coordinated. How many clothes must he have to own complete outfits like that? "Have you ever done any gardening before?"

He smiled at her then. "I don't know if you've met that amazing young lady that I came in with. I can assure you that as part of the many summers I have been visiting Sweet Blooms, my grandmother Delilah has shown me some basics about gardening."

Her gaze fell to his hands. She couldn't tell what it was, but Hannah put a lot of stock in how a person's hands looked. She found herself looking at his. They were moisturized, but she could see they had some nicks and scars on them. She knew he worked with wood; it boded well for him. Maybe this would work out well for her as well. If he stayed long term, she'd have some long-term income and be able to attract other renters.

What she needed to do was to be able to prove that she could make money from the house. That is if she wanted to keep it, the only home her son had ever known.

After she walked in, he took the knee pad and asked her where she wanted to start and what she wanted to do. When she didn't answer right away, he turned toward her.

"I take it you're wondering if I really know anything?"

"No, my crops are far enough along to take some rough handling from a rookie."

She went to the first row, got on the knee pad, and called him over. "I'm pulling weeds when I see them, and I have this sprayer that's full of water and tobacco. I use it to kill any bugs on my food."

"That's pretty smart. Most people don't know that tobacco is only good if you can apply it directly on the pest. What do you do for your soil?"

She had to give him credit for knowing that. "Later on, in the day, I'll take some cool tea and pour it out here. The caffeine will clear the pests and feed my soil at the same time. I have another knee pad if you want?" She pointed behind the gate. He went to it and then set up the knee pad across from her.

"Since you've set up so close, I assume you're going to want to talk about something?"

"Funny you should mention it, but I do."

"I don't suppose it would do any good to tell you this is not the time for any talking to be going on."

"Then I'll make sure to keep it short."

"Obviously, I can't stop you, so have at it."

"You seem to be a very straightforward woman."

"Mmm-hmm."

"Your point of view is a little distorted when you're emotionally involved, like the other day, but I can understand."

"You were one step away from being a pervert!"

"I caught you when you fell."

"But you seem to look past the fact I would not have fallen if I wasn't trying to hold my skirt."

"You can't deny I caught you."

She dug her trowel in the row, turning the soil. "Yes, you caught me after you made me fall."

"That wasn't so hard, was it? It was my pleasure to catch you."

"Oh, whatever." How much time had passed? He was starting to wear on her nerves. She tried to concentrate on the task at hand: her contribution to the cycle of life and caring for her garden. To further her efforts in ignoring the man beside her she admired the peacefulness of the house in the morning. How when the sun rose it caught just right and bathed the side of the house with light, and when it set it cast a warm glow over the whole property. Henry hadn't given her much, but every day she was grateful for this house and the place it had provided for her to raise Nathan.

If Nathan had been out here, he would have been groaning as they went along the rows. When she looked across the lane, Adam was keeping up with her as she moved along. For a good twenty minutes, they worked in silence with one another. When they got to the end of the row, they stood up, stretched, and went to the next row.

"You do this alone?"

"Sometimes my son helps me, but most of the time I do this alone. I can see you're better at this than you let on. If my son sees you, he'll try to make a trade with you. He's not as adept when it comes to gardening."

"Gardening is a simple pleasure I remember doing with my Grandmother. My father had a company out here once. He left and went to the city. I was still young, but I never forgot what it was to live here. My memories of visiting my grandmother helps to keep this as a special memory."

Hannah knew the story. Everyone in Sweet Blooms knew the story. The handsome Cade family, who were all good with their hands and made furniture. The father moved them to the city to make more money. Unfortunately, the business acumen wasn't as evenly divided amongst the Cades as looks were. The father had never been able to make a success of it and had passed of a heart attack.

Then Adam took over. It took three years of hard work and dark times, and then he turned it around and made it into a success. Adam not only breathed new life into the business, but he also brought in his brother and sister as well, so they all had a role. His mother had passed away earlier, and that was one of the reasons people said he didn't come back to visit his parents roots, because it caused too much grief.

"And have those memories brought you full circle to Sweet Blooms?" she asked. Would he tell her about the decision he made last night?

"I have to give credit where it's due. Nadia really brought me back to Sweet Blooms. I realized that wasn't the life I wanted." He stopped weeding and looked at her. "I'm going to be moving here permanently. To settle down. I want to join the city council and be a part of the place where I'm living."

Hannah had heard these things before. It was what Henry had said when they met. In the end, the city lured him back, and he left her and Nathan in Sweet Blooms. "You know Sweet Blooms is a great place to visit. You might find though, it's too big a change from the city."

He laughed. "Going to the city doesn't erase all of the knowledge that you have. I think I can appreciate both places for their merits, but I'm choosing to be here."

"I'm sure that will sound great to some women." She thought about all of the women who would see Adam and go all out to get his attention. "I'm sure you'll find that there are a lot of women here who will be interested in you. I'm sure it will make you a big attraction to the council as well."

"That was my thought, and I was hoping you could help me."

"Me?"

"A Jenkins has always been on the board. It's in the town charter because of the land ownership."

"Yes."

"I wanted you to take me to the meeting this week."

"You do know I'm the ex-wife of Henry Jenkins. They let me come because I live here. You should also know I'm not the most popular person in town either."

Adam shrugged. "I think between my money and your name, we'll be fine."

Hannah blurted out a laugh. "Okay, I would have never thought of it like that."

Adam laughed. "Believe me, when I walk into most rooms, people see my money. No matter who's next to me. They won't tell you to leave or give you a side eye as long as they think you're connected to my money."

Hannah looked at Adam and had to admit he was right. She never thought about people only looking to him for money.

"You're okay with them looking at you as if you're a walking dollar sign?"

"It's part of the package. I wanted to build a company my family would be able to live off, and there will always be those who think it just came to us without work.

As if building a company doesn't take sacrifice and commitment."

She reached out and touched his hand. "I keep a water bottle by the bench. Do you want a drink? It's a thermos, but I promise I change it daily."

"I would."

They went to sit on the bench. She took a deep breath, and her awareness of him became a tangible thing. She was on her side of the bench, but he sat with his arm on the back of the bench. With his arm stretched out his body pivoted towards her. She thought she could feel the heat from his arm lightly wafting over her shoulders.

She shook off her awareness of him and picked up the thermos to pour him a drink. Hopefully doing something different would take her mind off the position she was in. Handing him the cup she watched as he tipped it back and took a drink. When did drinking water become a thing for her? The real question was when had she ever seen anyone who looked like this drink water?

When he handed the cup back to her, she looked dumbfounded for a moment. She swallowed hard and blinked before putting the thermos on the side.

"You've lived in the city for a while now, yes?"

"Yup."

"I think Sweet Blooms is going to be a big adjustment."

"I'm ready. I've had my fill of the city life."

Hannah looked at him and wondered if he really understood what he was saying. She didn't want to judge him, but he sounded like Henry. She didn't know anything except what she had read and what had been said in town. While he seemed like a nice guy, she knew appearances could be deceiving. With her history of picking the worst in the bunch, she didn't think he would be the one to break her bad streak. He had the hallmarks of what she should stay away from. A man who lived in the city. A man who looked entirely too good. He had just enough good characteristics to make falling for him too easy. A man who brought his grandmother back to her hometown? That was too sweet.

Hannah hoped one day she would be able to trust a man again, but right now all the alarms were going off, and she didn't trust her judgment enough to know if she should be running towards him or away.

"Have you always lived here?" he asked.

"No, I've traveled a bit. I met Henry in the city, but when I came to Sweet Blooms, I knew I had found a home. There's something about Sweet Blooms you can't find anywhere else, good and bad," she laughed.

"The bed and breakfast?"

"No, this isn't my trade. In truth, I used to be an arts and crafts teacher in a school." She smiled in remembrance. "I started fresh out of college in the city. I thought I could make a difference and bring a little peace to a city school. Doing crafts and working with my hands to create for others always brought me a little peace and confidence, but it didn't work out that way. The city took more than I could give.

"So, I married Henry Jenkins, who had what I thought was a perfect life. He was born and bred in Sweet Blooms. Little did I know his dream was to go to the city, the place I was running away from. I got pregnant and didn't want to go back, so I stayed here while he went to find himself in the city. When I'm here,

I do a lot of online arts that usually provide pretty well for Nathan and me."

"There's a lot of undeveloped land in Sweet Blooms," Adam commented.

"You probably don't know, but some tracts of land can never be sold. If the original owner sells it, it goes to the town in some cases," she said. "It wasn't until recently that we had a real concentrated interest in our real estate."

Adam smiled. "I heard through the grandmother grapevine."

"Yes, the grapevine is better than a viral video."

He leaned back against the bench and looked at the sky. "I'm hoping it works to keep me out of trouble as well."

"I don't think you have a problem with trouble, Adam."

"I'm human. I have the same problems that everyone else has."

"Problems paying the rent?"

He smiled. "Yes, several factories seem always to pay late no matter what."

"Whatever. If you are so country-minded, what made you become a businessman, and why did you stay away so long?"

He sat up and looked at her. "You really want to know?"

"I asked, so yes."

"My father had kidney disease, and I needed to get the company working to take care of my mom, sis, brother, and him. We had no insurance coverage, and this was all I knew. My dad had put away some money for us for college, and he gave us the money.

I took mine, reinvested it in the company, and built it. After the money started coming in, we were able to pay for the increasing bills. I discovered I had a knack for it, and I kept going. As my siblings got older, they too tried their hand at some things until they found a place they felt they could thrive."

Hannah thought the Cades were all talented and gorgeous. "How long before you actually started making a profit?"

"I took over when I was 19. The first two years I barely managed to get it together, and there were times I got taken for a ride. Then after that, I knew the lay of the land, and we broke even. We were in a lot of debt by then. When I got it together after three to six years, we made a profit, but it went to my dad's bills. Then he passed. After that, we started to have a growth spurt, and my brother's designs really took off."

"There was a snippet in the Bloom Chronicles that your hands were insured. They said Nadia's body was insured as well. When the two of you touched, it was the most expensive meeting ever."

He looked at her with a crooked smile. "I never thought about it, but I guess so. I did the first designs that are used as models for the rest of the builders. Those original pieces are almost never sold unless we retire a line. It helps me to keep connected to the work."

"So, what will happen when you move here? You'll start building your house and do some farming?"

"Uh…no. I said I wanted to come home and settle, not come home and do the fast track to dying."

"I think you'll find that Sweet Blooms will bore you and you'll need to go back to your city."

"I'm not as dependent on the city as you may think."

"There are no gourmet shops here, no Broadway, and the restaurants can be counted on one hand. Much less the nightlife the city is famous for."

"I've done that already and having a home-cooked meal is priceless. I'm thinking of maybe teaching carving while I'm here."

"I think you have good intentions," she said. "When you look at Sweet Blooms, what you see is what you get."

He looked into her eyes for a moment before replying, "I like what I see here, Hannah."

Hannah broke their eye contact abruptly. She wanted to believe him. He sounded so sincere and sure. There it was again, the urge to believe his words. She looked away from his face to find his hand resting atop his jeans. The jeans that fit him to perfection.

Hannah thought of Nathan and reminded herself that she was often attracted to these snowbird type men. They would come to Sweet Blooms while they were contemplating life, but in the end, it was always the city that offered them that special something they couldn't live without.

"I hope you get what you're looking for," she said, and then stood up. "Well, I'll finish up the rest of the weeding."

She stretched and then went back to the garden.

"Hannah?"

She faced him.

"My gran told me you're the one I should talk to. I want to start my own business. You were right. I can't sit around all the time. I'll need to do something. I wanted to share what I know maybe in a craft class. I know you teach a craft class in town and wanted to know if I could teach with you?"

She looked at him and heard the caring and sincerity in his voice. In the early morning light when the day was brand new, she could almost believe him. In the beginning, it would be fine, but as the teaching sessions went on, he would certainly lose interest.

"No," she said. "It's too much for the kids."

He looked intently at her. "What are you saying? I know how to teach in small blocks. I want to get my feet back in working with people in a classroom setting."

"I'm saying that you're just coming back. You think you want to stay here. If you stay, it would be great, but for right now, I think you should know I don't think you are stable enough to teach."

Immediately, his face fell as he realized what she was saying. "You think I'm lying?"

"No, and that's the worst of it. I think you actually believe you can do it, and you would try your best."

Hannah didn't want to run off her only client, but she wasn't about to lie to him either. Dealing with kids was a precious gift. It was better to disappoint an adult than to put a child at risk. Hannah knew firsthand what happened when people left. Children were left behind, disappointed and scarred in ways no one could really fix. If Adam didn't understand that she had to tell the harsh truth for the sake of the children, then it was on him.

She heard him leave and didn't show him out. Instead she hung her head and let out a sigh.

She didn't go back to her weeding. The peace of the moment was gone. She picked up her tools and went back into her home.

Three

Sweet Blooms' General Store had a plaque when you walked into the store that said it was the same way it was when it had been opened 85 years ago. The store was owned by the O'Malley's, and there had always been an O'Malley there. It was open at 6 AM, and it bought products from the town residents in the form of trade, barter, and consignment. Hannah bustled in early that morning to pick up some books from her friend the owner, Skye.

Several tourists were walking around, and Hannah could see business was picking up. She wanted to get in before the morning rush, but she could see the morning rush was becoming a regular spate of tourists.

Sweet Blooms didn't have a lot to offer but there had been an article on the Sweet Blooms Café, and everyone had benefitted from it. As a result of the Café's sweets, the whole town of Sweet Blooms had a small but steady tourist season.

Skye waved at her as she attended a customer. As Hannah patiently waited, the bell over the door rang and she heard a group of teenage boys come in before she saw them. They were all bragging about which one of them had carved the better eagle figurine.

Hannah listened. She always tried to keep up with the latest expressions. It was one of the few points that she and Nathan laughed about. The boys kept talking about their eagles and the skill it had taken for them to create the curves on their work. Skye finally called her over and put the books on the counter and blew a kiss. Hannah laughed. As she looked at the titles, she shook her head how fast things were going. Things were changing and still staying the same. She knew her thoughts were going back to yesterday's conversation with Adam.

She shouldn't have left things the way she had. The whole conversation had been on Hannah's mind, and she could see that part of the problem was the anxiety she felt at having to tell Nathan that his father was going to disappoint him again.

The other part was that Adam made her think of things she had agreed she was done with. Being attracted to a man from the city was a recipe for hurt. Her snap answers were her way of avoiding pain, but she was working on it. She wished she could say it was to make her a better person, but it was really for Nathan. She wanted him to be a better communicator.

She knew she had to get past this stereotype of *city men*. More importantly, she had to get past the low self-esteem issues that made her think she would never be enough for a man to stay with. It was easy to write the declaration down in your book. It was harder to believe it was true when all the evidence said it wasn't. Her head knew the truth, but her heart was saying something different.

Between those issues and the town treating her like she was the permanent outsider who had bamboozled her way into town, she had to get it together for Nathan. She had thought about remarrying someone in town, but she hadn't found anyone she could imagine raising Nathan, much less being her partner.

She needed an answer. She picked up the books, and she noticed the boys weren't chattering away anymore. Then she heard that voice. She didn't need to turn to know who it was. The group of boys stood in front of him as he spoke.

"I want you all to know I'm really proud of you for making your eagles. We'll polish them up and then take them to be donated to kids. Like I said, if you finished the 8-week course you'd be able to go camping. Get whatever snack you think you'll need, and that a bear won't smell right away. Your camp guide is waiting."

One or two of the boys stopped. "Really, Mr. C?"

"It could happen," Adam joked.

Hannah saw a couple of the women in the store stop to take a second look as Adam strolled through the store. She told herself she was looking at the women fawning over him. If she were honest with herself, she'd have to say she couldn't recall what any of those women were wearing. In truth she had spared those women a short glance, but she was tracking Adam as if he was on America's most wanted list.

How could a man wear a pair of jeans and a short sleeve shirt and still stand out? It could have been the sculpted legs, the rounded shoulders, or the deep voice that just said come and talk with me. It could have been the confidence that he carried like his skin. He was setting all of her senses off.

She took a second look at how the town reacted to him. They greeted him as if he were their own. She had been in the store for more than ten minutes, and save for Skye, no one had smiled or even acknowledged her presence. A plan started to come together for Hannah.

It was madness.

It was crazy.

It was doable, and she just had to get Adam on board. As she was trying to figure out a way to talk to Adam, he spotted her from the door and walked towards her.

Hannah was mesmorized. It was butterflies in her stomach and a tingling warmth that shot out across her body. She was suddenly hyper aware of being a woman as she smoothed her dress down.

As she thought of what the teens had said, and his reply, she wondered if she'd jumped the gun about who Adam was. She fought with the council now because they had made assumptions about her. They'd seen her curvy chest, small waist, and long legs and knew the only reason she had married Henry Jenkins was to get his land. City girls like her didn't belong in Sweet Blooms, they thought. When she and Henry broke up, they thought they knew the reasons as well.

Hannah couldn't remember how many times she had told Nathan not to judge people. You never knew what a person had been through by looking at them. Had she been hasty to put Adam in a box? She'd done it as a form of defense against the new feelings of attraction he ignited in her. Hannah wanted there to be something wrong with him.

She turned toward him and waited for him to face towards her. For a moment she thought he would just turn away—like so many other people in the town—

and just ignore her. When he tilted his head to the side and regarded her, she went for it.

"I've been thinking on what we talked about."

One of his eyebrows raised and he leaned against the counter. She wished he would look at something else, or that maybe one of the teens he came in with would call out to him.

"You are making this so hard," she mumbled. "So, it's not normally a thing that I do, but I didn't have the information and so I did that thing I don't normally do, where I didn't give you a chance. That was wrong. I was wrong."

"We are going to have to work on how you apologize."

"I'm so rusty at it because it rarely happens."

"Yes, I can tell. That you're rusty at it, I mean."

"Really?" Hannah realized she was about to lose it again and tried to take a deep breath. "I'm making the schedule up, and I could add your class to the schedule," she said. "I'm going to have a condition that has nothing to do with you."

"I supply all the people with supplies, and I make sure it's always safe."

She stopped him and shook her head. "No, I'm not talking about that. I would need to take the class as well. Not everytime, and I might not be in there for the whole class, but I'll be in the first batch."

"Checking me out?" he teased.

Hannah smiled to go along with his joke, but inside she was a mess. "I don't check out guests. I will say this. I won't cut you any slack when you're teaching. I take all the classes seriously. If I put my name to it, I want you to be prepared to work. Are you okay with that?"

"So, no special privileges for the residents?"

"No. You pay for your room and board, and I provide you with my home and the two meals. You want to teach a class, and if you provide good one, I'll make sure you have a class to teach."

He smiled at her, and again the fluttering started, and the room became a little warmer. "I wanted to test the waters, Hannah."

"I don't have a price, Adam."

"I'm happy to hear it."

She let out a breath. "How many people do you want in a class?"

"I won't teach more than four if it's a beginning class in wood. It's about safety and supervision."

She gave him a smile and a nod. "I'm glad. I'll get the word out. I rent space, but I'll give you all the details so you can make sure it fits your needs. Okay?"

"I'm good with that."

"By the way, I'm sorry. I shouldn't have assumed because you have Cade looks and money, you would be callous."

The corner of Adam's mouth turned up. "I'm really liking you, Hannah. And no, you shouldn't have, but I'm glad you notice these Cade looks."

She rolled her eyes. "I'll make sure to judge you on what you present. Like that inability to take directions and a predilection to look up ladders—"

"Is that you trying to get me ready for settling down?"

"I wouldn't even try." She knew that once the women saw he was here for more than just a week, he wouldn't have any trouble finding someone. "I'm just giving you a fair shake on who you are. I know what it's like to be judged when you haven't done anything."

"Thanks," he said.

Hannah cleared her throat to try to break the moment. She was getting sucked into the Adam vortex, and she had to save herself. She vaguely recalled picking up her books and then telling him she'd see him later.

Once she was in her minivan, she was once again grateful for the tint on the windows. She laid her head on her steering wheel and tried to regroup. She had to face the truth. This was not a passing fancy. She was attracted to Adam, and not in a *I saw him in a magazine and could daydream about him* kind of way, but in a *man and woman* sort of way.

If anyone signed up for his class, she would be with him day in and day out until the course was done. It was going to be more than just *see you at meals*; it would be real interaction. Once again, her ability to be attracted to the wrong man was in full force.

Taking a deep breath, she pushed away from the steering wheel and braced herself against the seat. She was already thinking about how they could help each other. Why did that seem like a good idea? It that was before she knew she was attracted to him.

She needed to stick to the plan.

The plan was simple. She would help him find Ms. Forever—if she existed in Sweet Blooms—and he would help her become more socially accepted in Sweet Blooms. If a Cade said she was okay, then certainly everyone would accept them as okay.

For now, she was going to go home and do what she always told her son to do write your plan out and then put it on the side. If it still read and looked like a good plan the next day, then it was a great plan. Also, when she was nervous, she knitted, and tonight there was a scarf on the agenda.

Four

At some point, Adam knew he had to meet the council. The council at Sweet Blooms was a lot like the board of directors for his company. He might be moving out of corporate, but it seemed he wouldn't be able to avoid this. He wanted to be welcomed in the community and not become a financial pot for the community. Adam's thought was that if he established himself now as a business owner then he could begin to reshape the view.

Hannah had told him that he needed to present his idea to the council if he wanted to open in a building where zoning and licenses would come in. The Mayor of the town, Tamara Mason, was very involved in all the town businesses. Adam wasn't nervous, but this was a different environment than corporate. It all depended on him starting off on the right foot.

When he came into the room, he had to stop the laugh that bubbled up. They had given him a small table and the council member's chairs were sitting on a dais as if he were about to be judged by a council of royal towns people. Which was partially true. He took a seat and waited for them to make their grand entrance.

Adam smiled when he saw Hannah's face amongst

the council members. He was glad she was there. The members ranged from their late thirties to the more senior members. The Mayor he had seen before with his grandmother; they were about the same age.

He was surprised to be the only one in this meeting, but the clerk had explained that the presentation of new businesses was a closed-door affair and then the council would vet the idea first. Adam's curiosity was piqued as to why this process was in place, he would surely ask Hannah tonight.

Hannah was sitting at the end of the table. If it were possible, it looked as though the member next to her had shifted away from her. She'd mentioned the town judging her, but he could see he would have to take a second look. She sat in her chair with her back ramrod straight. She had her own papers, and she looked totally composed. His admiration for her only went up in lieu of how the council was treating her.

He remembered meeting her in the general store the other day, and it brought a smile to his face. Her emotions had flown across her face. She hadn't wanted to give an apology, but she did it because she knew it was right. She was a single mom in a traditional town. She stood up to them every day by having the arts and crafts classes, running a bed and breakfast, and being on the council. She was the type of woman a man could depend on. She had a lot of the qualities he admired in people. It came to him. That was one of the things that had been lacking between him and Nadia. They hadn't been able to depend on one another. People you could depend on could be your friend. They hadn't been friends. They weren't friends. He wanted his next partner to be his friend.

Mayor Mason sat in the middle of the dais. With a gentle clearing of her throat, both sides of the table turned towards her.

"This is usually the time we take care of in-house business. However, today we have Adam Cade here to present a business proposition to us. Before we do that, I'm passing out some papers to you so we can discuss two in-house issues first. The first one involves one of our own members, Mrs. Hannah Jenkins."

The Mayor passed the papers to both sides. She had her hair in a bun so tight Adam knew that was the reason she had cat-like eyes. She wore a sundress that was a very bright yellow, accented with a red scarf about her neck. Before she began to speak, she threw the scarf over her shoulder and straightened her back.

"I'm sure you all know that the Jenkins family home has been converted into the equivalent of a hotel. Mrs. Jenkins is receiving revenue for a person to stay overnight in her home with herself and her son," the mayor began. "When she was divorced from Henry, a judge gave her the Jenkins home for her son, Nathan."

"It's a good thing too, we all know that boy Henry came from bad stock," said one of the gentlemen on the council. "I knew Henry as a boy. He ain't never seen a dollar he couldn't lose. Now the boy done lost his pappy's home, and it's become a den."

The mayor frowned at the older gentleman, and he looked away as she continued to speak. "I can't speak on the character of Henry, Jerry. Henry is not the subject. The subject is whether or not the Jenkins hotel should pay lodging fees to the council like the other hotel in town does."

Adam noticed Hannah didn't say a word and he was beyond confused.

A woman in her late thirties who sported a hot pink, short-sleeved shirt with a deep vee leaned on her forearm and looked at Adam. "What do you think is going on in the Jenkins hotel?"

The Mayor cleared her throat, and Adam sat back as the woman in the pink shirt raked him over with her gaze. "Clarissa, do not address the visitor; this is internal business."

Clarissa sat back and pulled her top down, making sure her assets were displayed. Her smile widened and then she winked at Adam. He couldn't believe what he was seeing.

"I've spoken with Mrs. Jenkins, and in the packet, you can read her statement. She does not feel it should be treated like a hotel, so no revenue is due."

"That Henry boy is such a wastrel; not sure she has anything to give," Jerry murmured. "We should just let her be."

Adam knew small towns had their own way, but this was an education. If this was how they treated Hannah and she was a resident, he couldn't wait to see how they treated him. He was about to brush it off until he looked at Hannah with her head held high at the end of the table. Seeing her proud and strong, not saying a word, he knew he couldn't leave her alone.

"Ahem, I know I'm not a current resident, but I'd like to say—"

Jerry perked up. "The boy gets to speak?"

"Mr. Cade, I did tell you this was internal business," the mayor reminded him.

Clarissa leaned forward. "Please let him speak. His family has good standing here." The mayor acquiesced.

"Cities don't charge bed and breakfasts like hotels. My grandmother and I are staying there for her birthday. I can tell you it's not a hotel."

"Is she giving you bad service?" purred Clarissa.

"Not at all. We get wonderful meals, and the rooms, like any other bed and breakfast."

Jerry whispered loudly to Clarissa, "Is he saying he's not happy?"

"He's saying nothing is happening out there. More's the pity," she replied.

"Sounds like there's no money anyway," council member Loretta replied. She wore a blue and white dress and looked to be in her 50s. She leaned over to talk to Jerry at the other end. "Jerry's right; Henry wasn't a good boy, and I can't see how he'd be a good man, going off to the city any chance he could to follow them pipe dreams,"

"Ain't she from the city?" Jerry asked.

"She is, but she's living on the Jenkins place, so she'll get better," replied Loretta.

"Enough about Henry, please," the mayor interjected.

Jerry sat back in his seat. "I think Mrs. Jenkins is fine. She ain't baring her wares in town. Her son is a good boy; he helps me across the street."

Loretta leaned out. "How the boy acts is a good sign. We all remember how Henry was." After receiving a glare from the mayor, Loretta sat back. "I was just saying," Loretta mumbled.

The mayor cleared her throat. "I think we can all agree that Mrs. Jenkins is not running a hotel."

"She's not giving any service," Clarissa said with a sigh.

"That Henry boy is still no good," mumbled Jerry.

"She's raising that boy in a good Sweet Blooms kind of way," chimed Loretta.

"Then the issue of collecting has been taken off the table," the mayor said.

Adam didn't know whether to laugh or run up and save Hannah from the madness.

"Next business is the Parker Farm."

Adam knew of the Parkers. They had been one of the founding families. He even remembered hanging out with them. There were four of them and they all played hard and worked hard. If he remembered correctly, all of them left Sweet Blooms.

"The Parker ranch has become an eyesore. We can't sell it because the Parker boys are still alive. They have signed over the power of attorney and management of it to the council," the mayor continued.

"How is this an internal issue?" asked one of the other women on the council.

Jerry coughed. "It's bordering my place. The vermin are taking up residence, and they are getting so bold my old tomcats are scared of what's coming across the fence. We need to burn it! Just to level it, so there's no place to hide."

Mayor Mason's pursed lips suggested she didn't agree. "I wasn't thinking of something that drastic. I was thinking we could get someone to come to renovate it and open it as a working farm museum or something to that effect. I've seen that has been a great money maker in other towns. In this case, all the proceeds would go to the city treasury."

There was a buzz of conversation about why anyone would even come to the old farm. The Mayor held up her hands.

"I didn't expect we would resolve this today, but I've called a renovation expert and one of the Parker boys to look at the proposal."

"People will come for this?" Loretta asked skeptically.

Jerry shrugged his shoulders. "Those city folk are so weird. They'd probably come out for it."

"We'll bring this back up when the expert and the eldest Parker boy comes home. Now let's move on to our business proposal."

Adam stood up and walked in front of the table and started.

"First, thank you for seeing me on such short notice. I want to thank Hannah for suggesting I meet with you all." He gave Hannah only a cursory look, but it was enough to see the uptick of a smile.

"I assure you any of us would have been willing to invite you over," Clarissa said with a secret smile.

The mayor cleared her throat, and Loretta giggled like a schoolgirl. Adam kept his smile in place and started his pitch. He explained how Sweet Blooms was the home he never forgot, how he wanted to settle down here in peace. He had given control of his empire to his sister and brother and wanted to open a place where people could learn how to do woodworking. In a time when people picked up traditional hobbies it would be a great attraction for the town. It would provide entertainment for the teens, as his latest impromptu class had proven, and it would allow him a way to contribute to the town financially.

When he finished his presentation, the council was

enthralled by the story he had woven on the success it would be for everyone in Sweet Blooms.

"I can see you put a lot of thought into it, and the council is always interested in acquiring more revenue," the mayor said. "We have a couple of success stories in town as well that may be able to assist you."

"Thank you, Madame Mayor."

"So, you won't just be visiting, will you? I mean, you plan on living here?" Clarissa asked.

"That's the goal."

Clarissa licked her lips. "I hope you'll be able to find someone to settle with. You look like a city transplant like myself, please feel free to call on me if you need help getting your ideas together."

"Run, boy," Jerry murmured.

"I'm glad you want to give back to the town," Loretta said, her voice louder than it had been before. "I think there are other ways you can help and accomplish your task of settling in."

"Maybe not now—" Mayor Mason said through clenched teeth.

Loretta bent forward. "If you could endorse Sweet Blooms as a place that even you would settle down in, that would help us establish our town as the great place it is."

Mayor Mason looked pleadingly at Adam. "I'm sorry. When you came back to town, there were some rumors you might be staying. Recently, we've had a lot of interest in our lands from realtors. They've found some rules that say if we don't build the town up, they will nullify our land grants and take over the land as restoration and prevention of a health hazard. So, we're investing in building our businesses."

"And our name," interjected Loretta. Adam looked

over at Hannah's expression of shock. It was the only thing that helped him keep it together. He didn't know why, but if he thought she had been in on this, he would've felt betrayed.

He kept his smile in place and nodded as Loretta babbled on about what Cade Designs could do and how a man with his money could donate so much more. He didn't stomp out angry like he felt. Instead, he listened, every now and again looking at the clock.

"Well, that's my thought," Loretta finished.

The mayor could barely look him in the face. "We are happy and will help build your business. I'm sorry we went off the topic with regards to our Sweet Blooms promotion. I'll confess, we thought to ask for your input in the form of advice, not money."

"But your money sure wouldn't hurt," Loretta chimed.

<h1 style="text-align:center">Five</h1>

Adam got into his truck and started driving. His grandmother had thought it was ridiculous for him to rent a truck while he was here. Now he was glad he had done it. With the windows rolled down, he looked for the nearest open road and drove along. He needed the air in the truck to take away the heat of anger.

He was a businessman. He understood how things went. Everyone wanted whatever they could get. When it came to money, people he thought he knew changed. This wasn't the first time he had been invited to speak only to find he was being set up for a financial squeeze. People who had told him he would fail and never make it in the industry came to him now. They all had an agenda, and most of the time it was his money.

He'd made his fortune, taken care of his family, and dedicated his life to making sure they were taken care of. Now he was ready to do something for himself. His encounter with Nadia had proven to him that money could be a trap in and of itself. He was always so focused on taking care of his family after his dad passed away that he never gave any thought as to how it would affect his personal life when he decided to get one.

Well, the council sure showed him today.

"What am I doing?" he shouted, grateful for the rush of wind that carried his frustrated voice out into the empty highway around him. He drove down a dirt road that looked familiar and led to a pond. His dad had shown him this pond when he was learning how to fish.

He went around it and found the path he had taken Mary Jo to when he was in school. A smile came to him as he remembered how much he thought he knew. He had been ten, a fisherman, and could now kiss a girl on her cheek. The frustration of the council meeting started to dissipate.

He didn't think he just got into his truck and drove. He didn't clock the time or even think about going to a specific place, but he found himself in front of the community center building. Hannah said her classes, and ultimately his, would be on the first floor.

He looked at a sign labeled Sweet Ideas Center. Not the most original, but he could see someone was trying to keep a theme. The door was open. Inside he could see swashes of color on the walls. When he walked in, there was a guard at a desk. When he said he was there to see Hannah, the guard waved him in.

The center had an open middle room that led off to different rooms like the arms of an octopus. He heard a cheer and went to the viewing windows of one of the rooms and pressed a button beside it so he could hear inside the classroom.

Adam watched as teens, male and female, sat around a circular table.

"Okay, guys, the hardest part about starting is making the knot. I know there are tons of ways to make a knot, but we have to start our knitting with a special knot that we can hide later. We call it the pretzel knot."

The group looked confused, and when she passed out a cutout of a sourdough pretzel, everyone laughed. Some of the teens put the outline to their faces and looked out as if it were a mask.

Hannah clapped her hands, and the whole class came to attention. She showed them how to lay down the outline and take their yarn and make pretzels, and then slide their needles in the top holes. They did it several times with different needles—wood, plastic, large, and small.

He watched how she went from teen to teen. At one point she paired everyone up and made sure they all had it right. She waited until everyone was confident in the task and then moved the group to cast on their first stitch.

What caught his eye was the way one of the girls had a problem with her yarn. Hannah stayed with her until she was smiling over her work. She hadn't neglected the rest of the class. In fact, when Adam thought on it, he could see that Hannah was able to multi-task and make the individuals feel as though they were getting her full attention. The class was filled with laughter and ease.

He felt someone tap him on the shoulder. When he turned, it was a tall, middle-aged woman who gave him a bright smile. She mouthed *I'll be right back* and went into the room. Hannah looked up to see the woman and then saw him at the window. Moments later she was giving instructions for everyone to start cleaning up and putting their work away until the next session. The door was opened, and the kids came pouring out, but not before they had said goodbye to Hannah, and she had given each one a different word of encouragement for the day.

Adam digested the scene before him. He wanted to be a part of young lives like this. He wanted to be able to offer them something that would be their own. It would be a skill they could practice to destress or just to be themselves. Looking at Hannah had cleared away any doubts he'd had about proceeding after what happened with the council.

The woman leaned over to Hannah and spoke before walking toward him.

"Hello, you must be Adam Cade," she said, holding out her hand. She held a clipboard in her left. "I'm Sandra Waters. It's a pleasure to meet you."

"It's a pleasure on my side as well."

They shook hands, and he noticed her grip was strong and enthusiastic.

Sandra was in her mid to late fifties, with black hair and brown eyes. She was taller than Hannah and had a gleam about her that reminded him of Mayor Mason.

"The news is you're going to be settling down in Sweet Blooms," Sandra said.

"The news gets around quick."

"Hannah said you'd also be looking to teach here at the center."

"Yes, Hannah is going to give me some pointers and make sure I'm ready before I start officially."

Sandra's brown eyes narrowed, and she took a step toward Adam as if she were about to tell him a secret. "It can take a lot of patience to teach our groups."

Adam smiled. "I trust that Hannah will assess me correctly. I want to be able to give something back."

"Do you really want to give back?" she asked.

Adam could feel the cold mercenary hands of intent slipping towards his wallet. He knew what was coming but hoped he was wrong. "Of course."

"The center could use a cash donation," she said. "We make a small profit when people hold their classes here, but if we really want to make the center into something for everyone, it would have people like you invest."

Hannah stood by Sandra, hearing the words and hoping she wouldn't say them or at the very least do it way more diplomatically. She watched Adam to see how he would take it. She didn't see him change his smile, but his body tightened for a split second, and then it was gone. There she was again, her feeling bad for him. Adam may have come to Sweet Blooms to be the boy next door and find a nice gal, but he had a long way to go before the people could look at him like that. A man like him could build and open his own school to teach woodworking. Why would he go through the center?

Hannah had questions, and she was going to ask them. As soon as she stopped being so chicken and took the time to be alone with him and ask. Her thoughts were interrupted by Sandra asking for support. "Don't you agree, Hannah?"

"I'm sorry, I was thinking about the next class. We have two wheelchair students coming. I don't think I put the ramp down in the back."

"No worries. I'll go do it. Perhaps you can be more persuasive with Mr. Cade."

Hannah nodded as Sandra walked away. When Sandra was going towards the back, she faced Adam. "If you care about your pocket, you better leave."

Adam smiled. "My pocket is safe. You did that for me?"

"What?"

"I know you didn't forget to put the ramp down."

Hannah rolled her eyes and pushed Adam to the door. "Out with you, and don't think this was free. Meet me at the Banter House in two hours. I'm hungry, so be prepared to feed me real food, not salad."

Hannah loved the Banter House with their hand-made, oversized, cookout style burgers. The misshapen patties made her mouth water every time. The Banter House was that in-between place where you could bring your family or a date. The date part was the issue. Every move she made was noticed, and she was sure everyone would notice this one too. Being the object of gossip or scrutiny wasn't new to Hannah. As long as it didn't get to Nathan, she'd be able to ignore it like she did most of the other comments.

When she arrived, there were only a couple of people inside. The crowd came for lunch and dinner and she had made arrangements with Adam during the break time. Adam saw her and stood up, waiting for her by the booth. How was it possible that even his dark blue jeans looked tailored to his body? He had on a blue button-down shirt; the sleeves rolled up to his elbows. When he waved her over, she could see the shirt stretch over a chest that was comfortable at the gym.

Hannah was glad she had decided to put on her flower dress and flat black shoes. Not that she was all that concerned with his opinion of course. She just wanted to make sure she was maintaining herself.

The waitress came to the table, pulled out her pad and gave Adam a killer-watt smile. She turned her back partially to Hannah so there would be no doubt as to whom she was here to serve.

"Can I get you anything?" the waitress asked, obviously doing her best Marilyn Monroe impression of breathlessness.

"We'll have water first," Adam said and looked to Hannah.

For a second Hannah wasn't sure what he was doing, and then she looked at the menu.

"Oh, are you waiting for me to order?" He smiled at her and nodded. Hannah looked down at the menu. She knew this menu backward and forward. At this moment though, she couldn't see a thing. She couldn't remember the last time a man had waited on her unless it was to pay the check.

Hannah supposed she was taking too long because she heard the waitress say, "I'm available after shift if you're interested?"

She couldn't look up. If anything, she tightened her hands on the menu. She waited for him to accept. She'd understand, and somehow make it through the meal.

"I'm not interested," he said.

"I heard you were looking." She twirled her hair around her finger and bit her lip.

"Did you?"

"Yeah, my aunt's on the council."

"Ah, well, I'm not interested," he repeated.

"Your loss. When you're ready, Alice will take your order."

When Hannah was sure she had left, she looked across the table to see Adam looking back at her.

Adam shook his head and gave a mocking laugh. "I had it in my head that when I came home, everything would be the way I left it. That somehow the town would see me the same way my grandmother sees me," he said as the waitress looked over her shoulder one last time before handing the pad to another girl at the bar.

"I don't understand, Adam. You've come back several times. Each time you came, it was like the royal family had arrived."

"I thought people would be able to see me as a regular guy."

"I'm pretty sure the waitress saw you as a guy."

"The who? I'm sorry I was looking at the menu."

"The girl/woman who wants to be the mother of your children and will forgive you and take you on if you beg politely."

Then Adam smiled, and it went all the way to his sable brown eyes. "Okay, she didn't say all of that."

"She offered herself to you!"

"No, she offered to take my money off my hands. I have to tell you when I get random offers from women, I hear they are offering themselves to my money not me."

"I take it women offer themselves to you a lot?"

Adam frowned. "I don't know if I like the way that sounds."

Hannah looked at him and then at the women gathering at the bar. "I don't know how it sounds, but if you look to your right, you'll see there is a compilation of women preparing to offer you whatever you want."

Adam spotted the gaggle and picked up his menu. "Ignore it, they'll go away," Adam muttered. "What do you recommend?"

"Everything that says Thursday on it," said Geeta, appearing at the table on sandaled feet. Hannah couldn't remember a time when Geeta hadn't worked at the Banter House. She was from Lucknow, India, her eyebrows were always arched, her tone was always crisp, and she was married to Jerry. But no one had any idea how old she was.

"So, you're the man with the deep pockets and a nice smile. I saw you in the paper. The picture didn't do you justice." She looked at Hannah. "You taking up with him?"

Hannah choked and tried to clear her throat. "He's staying at my place."

"Hmm, we'll see. You two look good together—the outcasts." Geeta leaned on one hip and then nodded towards the menu. "I hope you're not one of those cheapskates. You want to sit; you need to order real food and a whole meal. No ordering appetizers either."

Hannah thought she was going to have to save Adam, but then Geeta turned to her.

"Sweet tea for you, Hannah?"

Hannah nodded.

Geeta turned to Adam. "And you?"

"Coke."

Geeta pushed the pen into the large topknot on her head. "Hannah is getting her burger with bacon and avocado on the side. She also gets sweet potato fries. Since you don't seem partial to anything else, you should get that."

Adam nodded and gave her a genuine smile.

Geeta gave him another long look. "I'm not saying you don't look good, but for Clarissa to mention your money before she mentioned how good you look you must have an awful lot of money. By the way, we take cash.

None of that plastic here." With that, Geeta walked away. When she was gone, Hannah laughed.

"Geeta is a permanent fixture of Sweet Blooms. She keeps us all balanced."

"Is that what you're calling it these days?"

Adam looked at Geeta as she passed by and winked at her before turning to Hannah, smiling. "Did I tell you I like her? She's the second genuine person I've met."

"She came to Sweet Blooms as a waitress, and about ten years ago she bought it. She's one of the first people who welcomed Nathan and me."

The pouty waitress came by and dropped off their drinks a few minutes later.

"So, I could tell you weren't thrilled with Sandra asking you for the cash."

Adam sat back and took a breath. "It's not just her. It's the whole day. First, it was the council. I didn't expect it all to break down to *I should give money.*"

Hannah sighed. "I wish I could tell you I'm surprised, but I'm not."

"The problem is, I expected this in the city. I thought it would be so different here."

Hannah saw him in distress, and the only thing she wanted was to help him past this moment. "You know everyone thinks you have it all. Even I thought you and your money were the same."

Adam pursed his lips and leaned his head back. "You're right, I shouldn't take it personally. I've got the money, and I have a life that most people want. It's fine. I'll give Sandra the money."

"Hey, it's still your money. If you don't want to, then don't."

"If I don't then—"

"If you don't, what will happen, Adam? Are they going to never talk to you again?"

He folded his hands on the table. "I'm trying to be a part of the town. It's hard to settle in if I'm not cooperating with the town. If I say no to everyone when the subject of money comes up, I'll be…"

"An outcast?" Hannah said with a humorless smile. "Listen, if you believe in the cause then go ahead and donate. If not, tell some of your other well-to-do friends. I don't think they care who gives them money."

Adam stopped. "I'm sorry."

"Sorry?"

"I didn't mean to bring up the whole outcast thing. I saw the way they treated you, and you don't deserve that."

Hannah swallowed the emotion that had come out of nowhere. She watched the concern and caring in his eyes, and it was too much. This whole lunch thing was becoming more than she bargained for. How long had it been since someone had thought about how it was for her living in a town that suffered her presence. Nathan had friends, but he was in his last year of junior high. The kids were getting older, and people would get meaner. She had hoped the town would at least accept Nathan, but Henry's antics coming in and out of town had divided people into believing either Henry's sob stories or the stranger who divorced him.

"You don't have to avoid the world. I don't. What I can tell you from experience is this: If you try to be whatever they want, they will always hold you to it. When you can't keep up the front, they'll make you an outcast because of that as well. So, you be you, and let them take you or leave you."

Adam leaned back in the booth. "How can I not take that piece of hard-earned wisdom?"

"What?"

"You're right. I want them to accept me, but I don't want to go back to living a double life like I was in the city. Thanks, Hannah."

"For?"

"For giving it to me straight."

"Well, that I can do, and it's no extra charge," she said with a smile.

"I don't know. If you keep it up—eating with me, giving me great advice—I'm going to start to think you really like me."

Hannah didn't answer. When the food arrived, it saved her from doing anything rash, like falling all over him in public.

"I'll ask a couple of my corporate friends if they're interested in Sweet Blooms. It wouldn't be the first time we've supported suggested causes."

"If you're interested in helping the center, I think it's a good idea. I don't know about the town campaign. I'd wait on that one if I were you."

Hannah noticed Adam had gone silent again. He hadn't touched his food, but he wouldn't stop staring at her.

"What is it? Do I have something on my mouth?" she asked.

"No, you're fine. You just remind me of someone." The smile had left his face, and there was a sadness in his eyes that wasn't there before.

Hannah knew it was a woman and she was coming up short. "I have to ask who?"

"Nadia."

"I thought you two weren't compatible." As soon as the words left her mouth, Hannah wanted to take them back.

Adam smiled. "I could see how you got that. I guess that means you missed all the good stuff of how we were Romeo and Juliet come to life."

"Sorry, I missed that part. After everything today, I don't want to put my judgments out there. It just seems like two people who have it all would have stayed together if they got along." She closed her eyes and groaned. There was no way she was making this any better with the words that were coming out of her mouth.

He gave a chuckle and then lightly tapped on the table. When she looked up, she saw him with a smile on his face. "Don't ever think you need to watch what you say around me. I'm grateful to have someone who doesn't mind telling me the truth."

Geeta came by with refills for their drinks. It gave Hannah a moment to regroup. If she was going to go forward with her plan of becoming more acceptable to the town by getting Adam to pretend, they're a couple, she needed to know more about Adam.

"Can you tell me about Nadia?" she asked.

Adam stopped his burger midway to his mouth. He looked at her, continued with his bite, and as he chewed it was as if the tension was leaving him.

"The funny thing is, you are probably the first person to ask me about Nadia. Everyone else had decided already and just accused me, or her, of one thing or another. Nadia is an amazing woman," he said with a smile. "Contrary to beliefs, she was born with her looks, and she started modeling as a dare in high school.

We met at a fundraiser. She was bored and asked if I really cared about the charity or if I was here to be seen."

Hannah took a sip of her tea. "I can see we would have gotten along just fine."

Adam laughed. "I'm sure. I would have been in trouble from two beautiful women."

Hannah just cleared her throat and let the comment go by. "And…" she prompted.

"And? There isn't much to tell. We tried to meet at functions so no one would know we were seeing each other. She didn't want to give up her place or things. I told her eventually when we were discovered we would have to make some decisions."

"Decisions like?" Hannah prodded.

Adam paused. "Decisions like having a family. I wanted a family. I wanted to provide for that family in a place that would be ours. Nadia had come from a poor family. It was so important for her to have her things. I was fine with it, but if we were going to be a family, I wanted it to be in a home we had purchased together as a sign of our new future."

Hannah stared at Adam. She could see this was important to him, and knowing he was a Cade in Sweet Blooms, it made sense that he would have such an attachment to providing and being such a traditional person.

"Then—"

Adam held his hands out. "You know the rest. We were discovered. The traveling was a mess. Everywhere we went we were hounded. I bought a home in New York. I brought her to it, and she said it would make a great summer home. She wanted to know when I would move into her large condo with security."

Hannah knew it was a bad time to tell him that maybe the place didn't matter as much as the people. Instead, she waited.

"Neither one of us would give. She couldn't let go of her past, and I had a future that I thought was worth fighting for. Throughout it all, she had been my friend. She told me how she envied people who respected me and not my face. That one of the reasons she couldn't give up her things was because her beauty would fade and the only thing, she would have left are those things to tide her over."

Hannah reached her hand out to touch his. "It sounds like you two had the same problems we all have. So much for the rich and the pretty having it easy."

Adam looked up and nodded. He placed his other hand over hers. "Thanks, Hannah. I didn't realize I needed to say that."

"I've got an ear for you to use whenever you want. I'm such a good person, it won't even cost you extra."

"Moving here to Sweet Blooms solves those problems and brings me in contact with family and friends. Speaking of which, I haven't met your son yet."

Hannah couldn't help smiling when she thought about Nathan. "He's almost 13, as he likes to remind me. This week he's away hiking, but he'll be back in two days. I actually planned it so he wouldn't be here for the week you booked. I wanted to make sure I could handle things."

"Smart woman. I've meant to talk to you about that."

"Yes?"

"My grandmother wanted to stay for another week. She's been so busy visiting friends we barely had any time together. Will extending the stay be a problem?"

"No, I'll even give you a discount for buying in bulk."

When Adam laughed, and he was relaxed, he was a force of nature. He made her feel safe, and she found herself leaning more and more towards the man. Bad luck didn't matter. All of her warning bells said this wasn't a forever man for her, but she could hear all the warnings fading into the background.

Time passed, and Geeta brought the bill. Without thinking, Hannah went to pay it, and Adam grabbed it first.

"I know you didn't mean to insult me, so I'll let you slide this time," he said.

"'Bout time a real man took her out," Geeta said from the side.

Adam nodded in her direction. "I do my best, ma'am."

Geeta grinned and waved him off. "I'm not giving you any attention. Already, the other ladies give you too much. But let me say, I think you've got a good heart under all that hunkiness."

When she left the table, Adam looked at Hannah trying to contain a laugh. "I don't know how I feel about being treated like an object."

"Don't think on it. Geeta is a law unto herself. Thanks for lunch."

"Thank you for coming out with me."

They walked out of the restaurant until he was at her minivan.

"So, I'll see you tonight?"

Hannah's mind blanked. "Um…"

"For dinner?"

"Oh, yes, of course." She needed to get in the car, turn on the air conditioner and pray no one heard him. She was just about to do that when he grabbed her hand. Hannah turned, hoping she could keep it together when he picked up her hand, turned it, palm, upwards, and placed a kiss on her wrist.

"Thanks, for everything," he whispered against her skin and then walked away.

She was dumbfounded. She looked at her wrist and thought *I'll never wash it again.* Her insides were going haywire, her brain was on delay, and the woman in her was rejoicing that she was still attractive.

So now she knew beyond a shadow of a doubt, she was attracted to the most unattainable man there was in Sweet Blooms.

Six

"Where are the tools?" Hannah asked, looking at the table of wood blocks.

Adam smiled. "Everyone asks that the first day they come into the class. I sent you the syllabus. You can see how close I stay to it." Adam had met Hannah at the center so he could set up. He was nervous and excited to show her the first lesson. "To tell you the truth, the first three lessons are about making sure we understand what we're working with and how to be safe."

Hannah nodded. "I saw that, and I was very happy."

Adam had given Hannah the syllabus after dinner. When she had finished going over it, she had asked him to give her a run through of a first class. She said she didn't want the whole thing but enough for her to see how he taught, and if the material was too complex for certain groups that came to the center. Now she was sitting on the other side of the table waiting for him to start. The moment brought back the early days his dad had taught him and his siblings about wood.

"Okay, let's get started. First, I'm going to talk about wood. It's important you understand how your wood is going to work and what it will and won't do.

The more you understand about wood, the easier it will make your life."

Hannah looked skeptical. "Wood?"

Adam hadn't noticed how her grin was so infectious. "I'm only going to do one fact with you. The first myth is wood is alive. It's not true. Once it's cut and sent to a kiln, then sent to the shop, it's dead. I brought in those three squares because they were once one square."

Hannah looked at the wood squares again. "They're three different sizes?"

"They are, because while it's true that a piece of wood is dead, what is also true is wood has a certain amount of water. These three squares were cut from a large square. One was put in a place that had a lot of moisture, so it expanded and/or grew big. The other square was in a very dry area, so it shrunk or lost its water and became tighter. The last square was left with the original woodblock by the tree. We learn about wood because while it's not alive, the environment can have an effect on our wood, and we have to take that into consideration when we use it."

He watched Hannah pick up each piece of wood and turn it around in her hands. Her hands were small and delicate. The wood looked large in her fingers. Her silence stretched on. He didn't realize how much her opinion would matter until this moment. She placed all of the wood down and clapped her hands.

"Well done. I hadn't realized that fact about wood. Having the pieces in front of me was great. I think you've earned a coffee."

A few minutes later, Hannah led him to the break room for the teachers. They were both holding a cup of flavored coffee from the Keurig. Hannah watched him over her cup.

"I've got to ask, are you sure you want to teach?" she asked. "A lot of people will come to gawk at first."

"I want to give something back to Sweet Blooms. I'm going to live here and raise a family." The thought of having someone to share things with weighed more and more on his mind. "I don't care if they come to gawk. As long as they take the class seriously, then it doesn't really matter."

Hannah shrugged. "I have to say I would have been one of those small-minded people who would have mocked you as well." Putting her cup down, she looked him in the eye. "I know what it's like to do your best and only have people see your mistakes, or even worse, they don't give you a chance and see only what they want to see."

"It's not my first rodeo, Hannah. When my dad passed away, I had to face that early on and let it flow past me."

"So, you're really going to stay? I find it hard to believe that a city person would willingly stay. Maybe this is just a mid-life crisis, and in a few weeks, you'll come to your senses and say, 'whew, glad I got that out of my system. I'm here for Nathan and the life I'd like him to have here.'"

Adam laughed. "Wow, your opinion of city people seems to get lower and lower. I've already wrapped up all of my condos in New York, so even if I wanted to, it's already occupied by another renter."

"What about the nightlife and the friends who would be up at any time of the day or night? Sweet Blooms is closed by ten."

"The internet and social media are amazing things. I have friends and contacts all around the world."

Adam knew Hannah was asking a bunch of questions, but he didn't know where they were going or coming from. He wasn't sure if the innkeeper wanted to know what his plans were out of curiosity or if she was asking like one of the women of the town.

Hannah and him.

It was an intriguing thought. He hadn't really thought about women at all since Nadia. People thought it was because no woman could compare, but the truth was, he was scared to put his heart into a new relationship right away. He had already gone through the phase where having people fawn over him was new and gave him a sense of power. Now he only wanted people around him that knew him, ones he didn't have to keep his fake face on for.

"You're right," Hannah said as she dabbed her lip with her napkin, "I'll make sure everyone knows I respect you. You know what you're doing in the class and, more importantly, you didn't buy your way into a class."

"Thanks, Hannah."

"I've got a class coming in. You know the way. I'll let you know when and where for your classes." Hannah stood and walked out of the room.

Adam watched her leave and noticed how she moved with efficient gentleness. He would have liked to watch her move that way a little longer before she disappeared outside the door. He liked watching the way she unconsciously flipped her hair over her shoulder and smoothed her hands over her lap as she prepared to go on to the next task.

He had to get a hold of himself. Was he looking at Hannah like a man looks at a woman? Adam took stock and realized that he liked Hannah, respected Hannah, and thought she was a spitfire in a cute package. He'd dated one of the most beautiful women in the world, but to him right now, Hannah's beauty was just as stunning.

Then it hit him like a ton of bricks. He liked Hannah, and it was more than just as the landlady. He was looking at Hannah as a potential partner in love.

"I'm sorry. I'm so sorry, but when he called, he said he had already worked it out with you," Pamela Jenkins said as she wrung her hands together. "You know I don't take sides in this."

Hannah laughed. "I would never hate you, and I know how persuasive Henry can be. Stop getting all worked up for nothing." Hannah stood in her ex-Mother-in-Law's house thinking about how this was not the way she thought the evening was going to go.

"Are you okay with this?" Pamela waited for an answer that Hannah wasn't sure she even knew the answer to. "I'll give you two sometime."

Hannah pulled her into another hug to stop the rambling and then guided her to the door. "Nathan will be here soon. You have fun at your game night with the choir members, and I'll see what I can find from Nathan."

Pamela smiled at Hannah. "Henry doesn't know what he missed."

"Off with you."

"I'm out and thank you for being so understanding."

Pamela had called her about an hour ago to tell her Nathan would not be coming home tonight and did she want to pick up his camping gear. Hannah was confused, and once again, Pamela and Hannah realized they had been victims of Henry's planning and not sharing. Henry had called Pamela and Nathan and made it seem as though him visiting Nathan this weekend had already been discussed with her. Henry often made plans with Nathan and got his hopes up before he discussed them with her. She didn't bother to correct it. Nathan needed his father, no matter how fickle he seemed. Hannah agreed to come over and figured she would wait to see him.

Now she was in Pamela's house, unsure of what her welcome would be. She and Nathan were having a complicated relationship on so many levels. She wanted him to be happy. He loved being in Sweet Blooms, but the drama from his parents was starting to leak into his life.

When he was younger, it was easier to ignore the snide comments of how she was a gold digger and how she had bamboozled Henry out of his family home. Children grew up, and high school wasn't going to be as kind as elementary school.

The wall in Pamela's house was a memorial to her family. Photographs littered the house from the surfaces to the walls of days when their family had been together. Henry had lost his father at an early age. There were fewer pictures after that time.

She'd always thought she would meet someone from the city, and they would be movers and shakers. They'd have kids, and they would be tiny movers and shakers too. Then she met Henry and came to Sweet Blooms. During their romance, she discovered she didn't really want the city life after all. The city of Sweet Blooms was the perfect place for children to grow up.

Neighbors looked out for each other, and the town worked together on existing projects and the direction the town would go. Now that came with the standard gossips, and generally nosy people, but as far as Hannah was concerned, those people weren't special to either city life or country life.

This year she had made a decision. She would marry and make a place for Nathan here. She was ready to stay and put down roots. She'd make this work. She'd give Nathan the one thing she didn't have: a home.

She was brought out of her reverie when she heard the keys in the front door. She went to the door and found Nathan dropping his backpack by the door. He saw her and went into her arms.

"Hi, Mom. Dad's coming to get me tomorrow."

"Hello, Nat. I know. I wanted to see you and just couldn't wait." She held onto him and took a deep breath of his dark hair. Her little boy was growing up.

"It's only been a week, mom."

"A week is too long in mother years."

Nathan wasn't getting any taller. It was a point that they didn't talk about and a pain point for him with the other boys. What he lacked for in height he made up for with smarts and speed. When he went into Junior High, Hannah had sat down with Henry, and they had decided to do whatever it took to help their son adjust in Sweet Blooms. Part of that was putting Nathan on a sports team. Henry was for it for all of a week. A week later the bills came in, and he made the discovery that sports weren't free.

Nathan laughed. "Mother years? How did the renter people go?"

"Well, they were real people from Sweet Blooms who came to visit, so it's been a dream."

Nathan grinned. "I can see it now. People will be lined up to rent for the week."

"I don't know about all that, but it's working out."

They both went into the kitchen. Hannah found some food and made Nathan a cold plate.

"How was the trip?" she asked.

Nathan tried to muffle his laugh. "It was fine. No one got hurt. It was good hanging out with the guys. They're going on a longer trip next month. I think I want to go on that."

Hannah listened as he relayed all the fun he had. Her mind was on how much the trip cost. She was already trying to move around paying things to make room for his next adventure. Eventually, the conversation came to the thing they both needed to talk about.

"You're seeing your father tomorrow?"

"Yeah, he said that we were going to go out and do something. Oh, he said I should bring some money with me."

Hannah wanted to stop and scream. Of course, Henry told him to bring money. It was blackmail, pure and simple. If she didn't send the money, Henry would sing that same old song on how he sends all that he can to her and then she and Nathan would have days of silence. Hannah hated having to put Nathan in that spot, and Henry knew it. It had to have been a good seven years since Henry had sent anything that vaguely looked like child support.

After eating, they went to watch a movie until Pamela came back. It was Hannah's turn to pick a movie, so they were watching what Nathan called a baby movie, but he endured as they watched. As Nathan sat next to her chomping on popcorn and looking at the Disney film, she looked at him.

"Hey, you told me everything about the trip, right? No more bothering the smallest but smartest member in the group?"

Nathan didn't answer right away. Instead, he popped in some more popcorn and then turned to her.

"It wasn't so bad this time. They still poke at me being small, but that's okay."

"But?"

"It was the same dumb stuff. There's going to be a father-son thing at the school, and some of them are getting together, I guess. They all know each other, so their dads knew, but I was just finding out. I'll ask dad about it tomorrow. Maybe you can ask him about it?"

Hannah reached out and pulled her son close. "Yeah, I'm going to call him tomorrow anyway, so I'll bring it up. Maybe he'll be free when they get together." The truth was she didn't care one wit, one way or another, what the boys did or didn't do. She also knew that Henry wouldn't come. The concern wasn't for her, it was for Nathan. He may not have said it out loud, but she'd heard her son in the middle of the night calling his father on his cell to come to the event. After he hung up, she'd also heard the sniffles that suggested his father had told him no. The fact that he wanted her to ask broke her heart into more pieces than she could count.

When Adam had gotten the text from Hannah asking if he was still up, he thought she needed him to go somewhere. She explained she needed to talk. It was almost 11:30. Whatever the talk, it must be really important. As he waited for her in the living room, he took a look around. The room was littered with strategically placed cameo frames. The frames held pictures of her and her son at all ages.

He'd already submitted all the paperwork for the class. According to the paperwork, the class would start in a few days. He hoped she hadn't decided to change the curriculum or try to move the order. He wasn't sure what it was, but he didn't want to pass up the opportunity to spend some time with her.

He had just taken a seat on the couch when he heard the keys in the front door. He didn't bother to get up because she was in quicker than he could pull himself to the edge of the sofa.

Hannah looked in the living room and let out a breath. "I'm glad you're here."

She came in and dropped her coat. She walked into the kitchen and then came out with two water bottles. Whatever this conversation was about, it was going to be tense. She was restless and gnawing on her bottom lip.

"Hey, what's up? Whatever it is, I'm sure there's some kind of solution," he said.

"I'm glad you said that because I'm counting on that being true."

She took a seat on the sofa and faced him. She just stared for a moment and then took another deep breath.

"Oh, fudge," she said, jumping up from the couch. "Do you mind if I stand while we talk?" she asked.

She was a ball of tension and stress. His concern skyrocketed. "Are you okay? Is something wrong with Nathan?"

When she looked at him, her face was the epitome of despair. "It could be fine. It might be great, but there are some things I have to fix, and I can't do it alone." She turned and walked towards the door, then came back to the couch. She plopped down on it and grabbed a pillow that she held in front of her like a shield.

Adam started looking for clues. She wasn't dressed any differently than she normally would be. She had on blue jeans that fit her curves perfectly—he was only slightly ashamed to have noticed already—and a floral top. There was no special footwear, just the same old sandals that she slipped her small feet in and out of as she pleased. He couldn't see any physical damage, and her hair was in its standard ponytail, exposing her long, slim neck. He didn't know what the problem was, but whatever it was, he couldn't see it.

He felt helpless, and he wanted to pull her into his embrace and tell her that no matter what it was they would be able to get through it. Adam knew he didn't have the right to do any of that. They hadn't made those statements to each other, and he wanted to respect her space. He knew she was here alone, so he was hoping the problem was financial. He had money. Adam thought about how much the property might cost in case the issue was her mortgage. He could pull it together quickly if she needed it.

"I need to ask you something," Hannah said, gripping the edges of the pillow. Every now and again Adam would see her fingers go through the fringe on the pillow.

"Ask, Hannah. Whatever it is, it'll be better after you ask."

"I think I need to give you the context first," she

said. She peered across the top of the pillow and closed her eyes as she took a deep breath. "I was raised in the city. My mother divorced my dad, and we all just fell apart. My mom has her own life, and when I didn't embrace traveling and living city to city, she decided I was too much like my dad, and she went on, and we remember each other on holidays."

"That's rough."

Hannah gave him a sad smile. "I didn't think it was the end of the world. I thought it was a sign. It helped me to focus on what I wanted. The idea came to me when I was young, and it held. I didn't want to have a broken family. I had associated being in the city with families that break apart. I know it's not true for everyone but…" She hugged the pillow closer to her and nibbled on her bottom lip. "I had it in my head that leaving the city and finding a "countryman" would be a safety against having a breakup. I wanted the dream so hard that I couldn't see beyond what I was sure was going to be the end goal. When Henry came by, he was infatuated with me because I was from the city. I thought he was the one because he was from a small town. He had roots. He could ride a horse. He was the whole package, so I did the only thing I thought I could.

"Ouch. You saw Mr. Right in the first one, and you got married," he said.

She nodded. "I did. I thought it would work out right. I knew we could make it work. He had all the qualities of the modern-day white knight." She drew in a breath and blinked back unshed tears. "You know, when he kept saying he wanted to go back to the city, I thought I needed to remind him of how great Sweet Blooms was. I cared for Henry. I can say it. I was so young that I cared for the life I thought I would have more. When I had the baby, Henry used that as an excuse to go to the city. He said the family property was a money pit. He didn't want to stay in Sweet Blooms. He said I didn't understand what it was like to live some-where and never be able to make a name for yourself. He said he wasn't falling for my tricks, and he left Nathan and me and went to the city.

Adam understood the appeal of the city and the country, and he knew that Hannah had been idealistic. It was the notion of a man abandoning his wife and son that made him angry. He understood duty. He understood having to put your dreams on hold to take care of the family. He had done it for his family. He didn't understand it when men left.

"He didn't leave you. He was running from himself." The words were the truth but still cold.

"It's like that saying, 'it's not you, it's me.' At the time I didn't know, and I can say I didn't take it well."

"You didn't take staying here well or—"

She nodded. "Yes, to all. I begged and pleaded with him. Then when Nathan came, everything shifted from my needs to his. I asked Henry to think about his son. He said the town would never give him a fair shake anyway. I realize the Jenkins' had a wild past, but when he was here, he and Nathan went places. The town embraced him and—"

"And you?" he asked. He had a feeling he knew how this had turned out, but still, he needed to hear it.

"Me not so much. I was the outsider who had tricked Henry into staying with a son. It's an old story. A whirlwind marriage followed by a pregnancy within the first three months and a couple that never got to really know each other. Then when he took me home. When we arrived at Sweet Blooms, they eventually started to tolerate me, and then I made a couple of friends. The thing that has always been an issue is, I'm not from Sweet Blooms. The friends I have are rebels, and I love them all. But I want better for Nathan. As time goes on, people will adjust to me, but for Nathan, Sweet Blooms is all he knows. One or two people are snooty, and I wouldn't worry, but they have kids Nathan's age, and I want him to feel safe and accepted. Everyone isn't a pain, but there are one or two who make my life and Nathan's, by default, a challenge."

Adam listened and understood exactly what she was saying. Sweet Blooms was filled with good people, but there were one or two people who could make it a bad experience. Nathan was just about to turn thirteen, and it was a big time in his life. High school would be coming, and in a small town, outcasts could be made in a moment, but you couldn't undo those impressions easily. Adam admired the fact Hannah wanted to give her son the best no matter what.

"I had considered other kids maybe," she blurted out. "Not with Henry, of course. We divorced, and then I became a mandatory eyesore because I was awarded the family house and Henry had to pay child support. Now they couldn't get rid of me, and everyone had to be socially polite but wouldn't invite Nathan to certain events because of one or two residents. It sounds bad, but you know the town is good. But one or two bad apples can make a difference."

"I think you're doing great so far. I haven't met Nathan, but the work in town, and even with this place, takes guts."

"Well, my motto is this: they may not like me, but they will respect me. I have to be strong for Nathan and me, and that helps me make it. However, I need to make sure I give Nathan the best chance possible. I want him to have the benefits of being in a small town. The close relationships, the role models, and the traditions."

"I can see you haven't let events deter you from your goal," he said.

"Good, I'm glad you see that because this is the part where we can help each other."

Adam was confused. "Help each other?"

"Yes, you need to settle without being hunted by every single person. You need to get a perspective to see how you fit without women throwing themselves at you and your money."

Adam nodded. It was true; he hadn't figured out how to be normal in a town that saw him as a walking check.

He wasn't sure what she was offering. Did she know someone? Was this a hookup pitch and he had missed it?

"Wait for it, Adam, I'm getting there," she said.

Adam smiled. "I'm waiting."

"We both have problems. I need to be accepted, and you need to scope out the land and people to find out where you fit." She took a deep breath and closed her eyes before blurting out, "I want to pose as your girlfriend. It will help me with the acceptance in town. If I'm your girlfriend, then you don't have to worry about offers, and you can teach and take your time settling in and looking for a wife if you want."

"You think that will help, you being with me?"

"Yes, I think you are the returning hero, and no one will say no to you. If I'm with you, then they'll have to accept Nathan and me. When we break up, I'll still be respectable enough to talk to. When you are with me, you will have fallen for the same city charms Henry did, and it would be enough for them not to talk to you or badger you about going out."

"So, how long have you been thinking about this?" he asked. He could see her logic. It was so Sweet Blooms. Once again, he was amazed by her thinking.

"You saw everything from the board to how and who Nathan hangs with being affected. Nathan needs a solution."

Adam was glad he was sitting. Hannah had come up with a plan to help herself and her son. She was thinking out of the box and still holding on to her dream about small towns.

"Listen, I'm not hoping we fall madly in love. I get this is not that kind of relationship. I just want my son to have a place and maybe get the chance to start over with someone here. I have a place, and it's big enough for me and another."

Adam knew this must have come at a big cost to Hannah. She was an independent woman, but for her son, she would make herself vulnerable and go into a relationship understanding nothing would come out of it. He had to say this took the cake of how a woman would ask to start a relationship with him. Adam thought he had seen it all. Women in cakes, messages, fake love children, long lost families, and even blackmail. None had come to him with a cause.

"I want you to think about it," she said softly.

"I keep thinking I need to find Henry. I don't think

there is ever a good reason for a man to abandon his family."

She peeked over the pillow and smiled. "Oh yeah, I can see your white hat."

"Well, that is one of the requirements for this to work." Adam looked up at the ceiling. "I need a moment before I decide."

"Please do. I understand it's a lot to take in. Believe me, I know it's a lot," she said as she swallowed and looked away.

Adam looked at Hannah and thought about her. She was fearless. If nothing else came from this situation, at least he realized she loved with abandon, and she gave everything to those she loved. Hannah probably didn't realize how strong she was or how courageous.

"Let's talk tomorrow," he said as he stood.

"We live in the same house, so it won't be hard to find me."

Adam nodded and left to go upstairs. By the time he got to his room and closed his door, he was beating himself. What was he thinking? He should have said no. He didn't say no because when he thought about saying no, he saw Hannah's face. He saw her face going toe to toe with him in the garden. He saw her holding on to that pillow but putting herself on the line to make a better place for her son. He knew where his thoughts were going, but he would sleep on it, and tomorrow it would be clearer.

Seven

After a fitful night, he was more than ready for the good news that came via email. Adam had asked a realtor to find the original land his father owned in Sweet Blooms. This morning he was told they had found it and bought it as per his request. This morning he was going to see where he would be building his new home.

He was used to rising early to get to the office early. This past couple of days had destroyed his schedule. The first couple of days, waking up late was great, but then after that, his body was recharged and started waking up on time.

Now he was ready to tackle a new project, and his new home was right on his agenda. His grandmother was going out with friends again today. She hadn't spoken much last night during dinner, but he made a mental note to speak to her while she was meeting her old friends. Hannah had already left, and Adam was a little ashamed to admit he was grateful.

That made him free and clear to go to his new home site. The site was more like a ranch. It was also run down. When Adam arrived, he was met by a smiling real estate agent who told him he was the only one asking about the property. Real estate moved very slowly in Sweet Blooms. Adam gathered that fact from the realtor. He was dressed in a white shirt and blue jeans. Hanging out of his back pocket was a rag with the company logo on it from a diner.

Adam had been on the property for about two hours, and he had decided to start with the house. It was old and needed a lot of work, but when he was done, it would be his. After two hours of putting in labor, he stood up in what he thought would be the living room. He had taken out debris, pulled down any loose sheetrock, and made notes on how many of the studs in the wall would need to be changed out. His hands were raw, his back was sore, and he had sweated through his clothes. It was a great day.

He looked around the room and thought about the sheetrock and insulation he would need. But what really caught his eye was the floor. The floor was its original wood. He could get up early and come here to take care of the house between classes. He had talked about getting his home set up. It was something on his list. His grandmother had suggested he find the old property and see if it was still for sale. It was on a decent plot of land, and it was big enough for him and his future wife and a couple of kids.

Adam looked around and thought about how far he'd come. He wasn't with the company. He was in his home. Nadia had told him she just wasn't brave enough to give it all up. Adam wondered if she had seen Sweet Blooms if she would have changed her mind. He knew they weren't destined to be husband and wife, but he still considered her to be a good friend.

He could fondly look back at that time and see they

had both needed a friend more than anything else. After their breakup, he had decided he would pursue the normal life with as much vigor as he did his business. He wasn't interested in someone who wanted him for his money. He didn't want to play the *let's go out and be seen by the paparazzi* game either. Nor was he interested in the dating game.

As he walked through the house over the dull bare wood, he found himself thinking of Hannah. He could admit to himself he had been avoiding thinking about what she had proposed.

He liked her. Hannah was a breath of fresh air.

Where others might pull their punches and say something nice, he knew she'd be straight. She'd already shown she was tough to stand up to whatever others might say about her. She was very competent and practical if the way her classes filled up were any indication. He could admit he was attracted to her as well. The issue was with him. He would do what? He would walk around with her, and it would erase what the town thought?

He walked out the front door to the little porch. On it was a folding chair, and he took a seat. Face up, he took in the warmth of the sun. It was different doing that here than behind the windows in the city.

At his heart, he agreed with Hannah. Sweet Blooms was a great place to live. Save for a few bad apples, it was friendly, and for kids, it was a safe zone where everyone knew everyone and watched out for each other. What Hannah didn't understand was small-town dynamics. His father had been active in the town. He had helped build roofs, participated in camping trips, and volunteered at barbecues.

She didn't understand that to become a part of Sweet Blooms; they'd have to go out together. Be seen by everyone. He knew there would be some events he'd have to do with Nathan as well. This wasn't a dog and pony show; it was about becoming part of something bigger than you were for safety. He knew she wanted it, but he was pretty sure the way she spoke and asked, she just didn't know what that entailed.

Could he do all of that with her? He was already attracted to her; if he did it, would it really be fake? He leaned over and picked up a scraper he had left outside. His thoughts were going towards helping her out because, at the end of the day, he thought that maybe both of them could help each other out.

"Are pigs flying?" Lucy said as Hannah walked into the spa. She laughed at Hannah as she rolled her eyes. "Okay, come on. It's lunchtime, and I'm free for the next two hours. Then it's the beauty queen of the council's seaweed wrap! Come, come and tell me. I've been waiting in suspense. Do you finally want to try the full body waxing?"

Hannah had been friends with Lucy since Nathan was born. When she'd first come to town, Lucy had explained to her that the spa made most things go away, even the comments of one or two mean women. Lucy was also a transplant to Sweet Blooms. She hadn't had the hard time Hannah had, but she'd had to make peace with the council. When she first came, no one wanted a spa, but she won them over, and now you couldn't tell she hadn't always been here.

Hannah walked in and laid down on the massage table.

Lucy gave her a smile and then raised her eyebrows. "Now this is a tease. Are you giving me permission to trim those brows or work on the knots that look like boulders in your shoulder?"

"I need my friend to listen to me and tell me the truth," Hannah said.

"You've always had that," Lucy said, pulling up a chair to sit down. "The fact you have to ask that tells me this is really big. Is Nathan okay?"

"It's huge," Hannah said slowly to her friend. "Nathan is fine. I've made a big decision for me," she started, hoping that Lucy would understand what she was about to say. She valued their friendship and, more importantly, Lucy had earned her trust.

Lucy reached out her hand and covered Hannah's. "Hey, I'm here for you," she said gently. "You want to tell me something. I'm a friend; that means I don't judge right away, and I do whatever puts your interests first."

Hannah laughed. This was why she came to Lucy. It was also why Lucy was so successful at putting everyone's fears to rest. Lucy had a way of coming to her aid in public and providing a shoulder for her to lean on when things got bad. She never turned her away, and she and Skye were Hannah's best friends.

"So, my news," Hannah started. "I know I need to say it, and it will be easier, but…"

"But, what? What could it be, Hannah? A tattoo, a piercing, or you've decided to date online?"

"No! I decided to take action on the acceptance thing here at Sweet Blooms."

Lucy knew about all the hardships Hannah had to deal with when it came to one or two people in Sweet

Blooms. They were like annoying thorns. She had organized a party with Skye for Hannah. She always told her the truth and was the first one to jump to her defense. While Lucy would tell you the truth, she also knew when to stay quiet if she thought you weren't ready for the answer.

"I asked you if you were willing to join the herd or make the herd like you. Did you decide?"

"I think I found a way to do both," Hannah said. She had no idea why she had laid down on the table. Now she wanted a pillow to grab or something to do with her hands. "I've come up with an idea."

"Okay, I'm all ears."

Hannah closed her eyes and then peeked out of one of them to see Lucy sitting with a smirk on her face. "I asked Adam Cade if we could pretend to be together. I would get the benefit of being with one of the more respectable people in town. No one would say a thing to me or exclude Nathan. He is looking for a good woman in town so he can see their true colors when they are around me."

Lucy's mouth opened, and her hands went to cover it. She looked like a cartoon character. If it had been any other time, Hannah would have laughed.

"Fortune 500 Adam Cade?"

"Yes."

"Mr. Daddy Warbucks Comes Home Cade with the hot looks?"

Hannah nodded. "He's staying at my home. I told you I was doing the bnb thing. He wants to settle in Sweet Blooms, and he's going to be teaching a class in woodworking. He's a nice guy really. We've been talking, and I think we can help each other."

Lucy fanned herself. "If I had known, I would have talked to him." Lucy cleared her throat. "I will give you this—when you pick, you don't low ball."

"You know me; I don't care what he looks like. I just care about his heritage here in Sweet Blooms. I don't really interact with anyone in town, so socializing like that would have taken forever. I didn't want a bunch of men coming and going in my house. So, I asked, and I'm waiting, and I'm here because you are the only one who would be able to tell if I did something beyond dumb."

"First off, you are a lot of things, and dumb isn't even on the list," Lucy said. "You came here and tried to make a home. You did classes for side money, and it's been getting some good traction online. You opened your home to be here for your son and make some more money to support him, and you did it all without Henry. You're alone, and you make decisions that you need to. So, do I think it was ill-planned? No. However, I think we need to be clear about what is really needed. Your problem is with a few who don't see you as a working part of the town. People are scared of change and what they don't know. You are both of those in a pretty package."

Hannah sat up and blew out a breath of relief. "I know. I'm working on it. What I figure is when I'm with Adam, I'll figure that out. Nathan wants to go to an outing with the guys. I can probably pay Henry to go, but I need to know when. I want Nathan to have the best experience."

Lucy chuckled. "You've got it all worked out. Well, that's your way. See a problem and make a solution."

"I would have agreed with you, but this is different. I just need him for a little bit, and it will be fine. Nathan will get the best I can offer him," Hannah confessed. "Adam hasn't given me an answer. I know it was a desperate plan. I wanted something, as did he, and I tried to present it in the most matter of fact way."

Hannah had played that night over and over in her head. She hoped she had said everything right. She could have not been hiding behind her pillow. Maybe she should have been more assertive. She shook her head. It didn't matter. It was done. Whatever was going to happen was going to happen.

"Do you find him attractive?"

"Adam Cade? He looks like he stepped out of the dictionary under handsome," Hannah said with a grin. "I think I hear where this is going, but it doesn't matter. I'm interested in his lineage, not his presence."

Hannah laid back down. "I'm not trying to rope me a millionaire. I just want to get to a place where it's comfortable for Nathan. I can get through it for Nathan."

"Okay, although you do make it sound like you're about to be sacrificed on the altar. Looking at Adam Cade, I know a couple of women who would offer to be the sacrificial lamb for you. At any rate, what's the next step?"

"If I knew, I wouldn't be on a table," Hannah moaned. "He hasn't given me an answer, and I should have an answer for each response."

"Well, if he says no, there's no problem; you ignore him until he leaves. If he says yes, then you two need to prepare to be the toast of the town."

Hannah raised her eyebrow at Lucy. "Us being the toast of the town? I don't think so. I just need him to do some manly bragging, and we should be fine. I'm wondering if there are any big town events that I should go to. I mean, I go to events as a council person."

"Well, you will still be going to events, just on Adam Cade's arm. Be yourself, and I'm sure you and Adam will work it out."

"Be me? Maybe I—"

Lucy grabbed Hannah's hand. "Listen to me. I know you have this vision and dream in your head, but you do know you need to be happy with you. There will always be someone in town who doesn't like someone. Consider this: you teach others how to treat you. You need to know you are good enough to be here too."

Hannah squeezed Lucy's hand back and blinked back tears. "I'm getting better every day. I just don't want Nathan to miss out because of me."

"Breathe. You're waiting on pins and needles. It's not every day a woman propositions a millionaire. I mean, every time we see it, it's vice versa. On top of it all, go in with a plan."

Hannah nodded. "When he says yes, I'll go over the where and the when."

Lucy smiled. "It's when he says yes now?"

Hannah sat up and threw her legs over the side. "I'm doing what you said. If I say there's only one answer, maybe he'll get a clue as well."

"Do remember he is a grown man. He may have an idea."

"As long as it goes along with mine, we'll be good."

"Yeah, that sounds like a great plan to tell a Fortune 500 company leader. Let me know how that goes."

Eight

Hannah hated waiting. The fact that she hated waiting was exacerbated by the fact that she and Adam hadn't been able to meet up. She thought she would meet him at dinner, but he had been spending the last two days working on his house. Tomorrow Nathan was coming home, and she wanted to have this wrapped up one way or another.

She was back in her garden doing the weeding. Hannah had decided to fall into her work. She had long ago forsaken the knee pad, and her jeans were stained. She'd taken off her blouse until she was down to her tee shirt and a wide-brim straw hat that sat on her head. She had dug the trenches, filled them with food, and watered her plants. Standing to look at her handiwork, she smiled and then she jumped when she heard Adam clear his throat.

He looked like he had just stepped out of a vacation ad. He had on a blue shirt that was open at the vee of his neck. He had on dark jeans that clung to him at the waist but seemed to flare out in a boot cut from mid-thigh to the bottom. She felt an errant trail of sweat on the side of her face and went to wipe it.

She immediately regretted it, knowing her hand had probably left a trail of dirt in its wake.

"Yes?" she quipped. Frustration had her answering like a shrew.

Adam laughed. "I thought you loved gardening."

"I like to keep myself busy."

"I was trying to be friendly."

She wiped her hand on her jeans. "I find gardening to be a time when I can usually lose myself in work. It's something that can be tedious but must be done meticulously if I want to be able to eat from my garden."

"Aha. Well, I wanted to talk to you inside if you have a moment," he said, opening the gate so she could go to the house.

He was going to tell her one way or another. She was so tense that she didn't say anything. She couldn't go curl up on the couch. Instead, she found a chair with plastic seat covers and sat in that. Adam smiled at her fondly as if he just noticed that she had dirt everywhere on her. He pulled up a chair as well.

"Okay, now what?"

Adam looked amused by her impatience. She sighed, waiting again. He just looked at her, and Hannah began to squirm.

"I hope this is going somewhere," she said.

"Well, the first thing I know is your good nature starts to go out the window when you have to wait."

"Kick rocks!"

He laughed then. "Oh yes, I can see it results in questionable language as well."

Hannah crossed her arms over her chest and held on to her sides. She wasn't at her best. Why had he come now?

She had been making herself available at the house, looking all delicate and sweet smelling, but no, he caught her when she is trying to work off some of the nervousness.

"Waiting isn't a strong suit, and it could be identified as a habit only an indecisive person would have," she snapped.

He went to the small bar in the room and looked at the bottles. After picking up a couple, he turned to her. "There are a couple of wines, whiskey, and some sweet liquors."

She looked around him towards the bar and nodded. "I'm glad you can read. I hear it's fundamental."

He went back to the seat he had pulled up in front of her. "I'm asking questions is all, Hannah. I am not torturing you."

He sounded like silk, as he sat in front of her. It could have been one of her friends talking to her. Well, if they were totally gorgeous, a man, and happened to be a millionaire. This exchange was nothing for him. For her, it was just a lead up before the inevitable happened.

She was a strong woman. She took care of herself and her child. She dealt with her ex the best she could, and she kept her composure. All of that she could and would do, but this one-on-one conversation had her on edge. Hannah could hear Lucy's words coming back to her. The issue wasn't the town; it was her. Taking a deep breath, she tried to re-center herself.

"Yes," she said slowly. "I like some wines, straight whiskey, and sweet Amaretto to go in orange juice."

"No pretty drinks? Nothing with lots of ice and some color?"

"The point of a drink is to relax, and for it to be tasty. Those pretty drinks hide the liquor, and you end up being foolish or have no taste. I prefer things straightforward."

Hannah was screaming inside. What was with the questions? Would he do it or not? Why was he dragging this out?

"Adam, what are you doing?"

"I thought I was trying to have a conversation with a woman," he told her. "Sweet liquor can go to a person's head quickly, and most people have a challenge drinking that whiskey."

"I'm not like most people," she said. "When I'm having fun, I'm having fun, and when I'm working, I'm working. I like things black or white when I work and when I play.

"Do you think I'm lush or that I drink too much? I can tell you those bottles have been there a good six months, and I usually have to give the wine away or cook with it because I don't want it to go bad."

He leaned back in his chair and looked at Hannah. "I'm not accusing you of anything," he said softly.

"Good, because I'd have to set you straight."

"I think you feel like you have to set a lot of people straight about their thoughts about you."

"I do."

"You don't."

"What?"

"You don't have to defend yourself all the time."

It was the first time she had heard that from anyone. It was the first time she realized that she needed to hear it from someone. She got up from the chair and opened the small refrigerator that was below the bar. She took a small water, opened it, and took a drink.

"Hannah, I want to know about your family. The only thing I know is you're not from Sweet Blooms."

She took another sip of water. "I'm not clear why you need to know."

Adam held his hands up, "I'm not the enemy here. I'm just asking social questions."

"Okay. I have two siblings, a mother, and a father. My mother loves the city. I never knew my father." She thought about growing up in the city with her mother and having no dad. Father's Day was a cruel day for her. She had been the smallest in the class, and for the in-group, she had been easy pickings. "My mother worked all the time. She was convinced we were going to be rich one day. She would stay up and watch those late-night shows on how to make it rich with real estate," she smiled.

"Eventually, my mother decided to marry out of her situation. I don't agree with it, but it works for her. We don't talk as much as I'd like. We've probably always been more friends than mother-daughter." When she thought about her siblings, the picture grew dimmer. "My siblings are from my mother's second marriage. We talk, but we're not close."

Family dynamics were fluid. Some days her siblings remembered her, and some days they didn't. Sometimes they wanted her advice, but most times they called when they needed money.

"You don't see them?"

"No, and when I do, and they leave, I'm a little lighter in the pocket for it." She saw him lean back in his seat.

"You've always been this honest?"

"I've always been straight to the point. My mother

would say I don't have womanly tact. My mother is beautiful by society's standards. She is petite, soft-spoken, and shapely. When I arrived, we discovered very quickly I was not soft spoken. I didn't know how to not get dirty, and any shape I have is a side product of my working. These things have stripped away the need for me to be anything less than blunt."

Adam sat there and took in what she said. Hannah didn't know what he was thinking, but he kept his gaze on her steady. She knew what a bug felt like under the microscope and she wanted to get up and pace out of view.

"I appreciate honesty. It makes business deals go smoothly, and it helps to head off any problems that might occur," he said. "Contrary to what you might think, a lot of people like you and admire you. I think you don't give yourself enough credit. If the town was shunning you, as I think you believe, your class would be empty. I hear there is always a waiting list for young and old in your knitting classes."

This was too close to home from him. She could have endured this from Lucy or Skye, but with him it was personal. "You wanted to find out how bad it was before you spoke to me?"

"I did what I always do. I don't make decisions based on my feelings. I don't start anything I'm not pretty certain I can't finish and win," he said with a smile and a wink. "I'm saying yes to you, Hannah Jenkins."

She heard the words but didn't believe them. Her thoughts scattered to the four winds and then came back like a hurricane. He had said yes. He was going to help her. She knew she should say something. She didn't think he would it. She couldn't have imagined this moment of elation and fear colliding at the same time.

"After your checking up on me, why would you do this?" She wanted to close her eyes and just fall into the ground. Did she just look a gift horse in the mouth and then turn him away?

Adam wasn't deterred if the smile on his face was any indication. He got on his knees in front of her and put her hands in his.

"You've got fire in you, Hannah."

She didn't know what that was, but him being on his knees in front of her, holding her hands, was sending her into a tailspin.

"Fire burns everything and everyone around it. It sounds good now, but when the people start coming to you about me, you'll change your mind. I was wrong. I shouldn't have asked you. You're building your house. Building your tomorrow and—"

She stopped talking and looked at their hands. Then she looked at him and cocked her head to the side. "You've still got my hands," she said. He hadn't moved them or himself. Her hands were held in place and swallowed up by his. She could feel the random callouses on his hands.

"I'm good with what you want," he told her.

"Really?"

"Yes."

"Then I owe you a big thank you. Now that we're here, I guess I didn't really expect you to say yes. Recently, I visited a good friend of mine who said this problem I have might not be the problem I'm saying and—"

He stood up and sat back in his seat. "I know the

problem, Hannah. I'm offering to help you. If you feel like you're not ready, I understand."

Hannah wanted to yell 'no, I'm not ready.' Who's ever ready to face their inner fear out in public? What happens if he's with her and they still snub her? If they see that she's just not making the cut? Lucy was right. It was her and not the town. Yes, there were issues with town gossip, but the rest was…her.

She needed to garden or to do some heavy construction that would take up her attention and exhaust her body. She needed to–

Adam cleared his throat. "Hannah, I've got you. Focus on me." He reached out his hand for her to take. Hannah knew that Adam wanted her to take that hand. Take that hand and do what? Take that hand and say yes to her crazy scheme. She wouldn't remember standing up. She wouldn't remember moving to him. She wouldn't remember putting her hand in his. She would always remember the moment when his hand closed over hers.

He stepped closer to her. All of her thoughts scattered. She could see the blue shirt and the three buttons in the vee. She moistened her lips, then looked up into his eyes.

"From now on, we're a team," he said. Hannah numbly nodded. "The way this works is they have to get through me before they get to you or Nathan. Are you good with that?" Again, the acquiescing as she was pulled in by those deep wells created by his brown eyes.

She saw him leaning, and she didn't move. When his lips touched hers, she leaned in, and just as quickly as it started, it was over. When she opened her eyes, he was looking at her. He let her hand go and took a step back. "Partner, if we are going to be together, we have to be comfortable with each other."

"Comfortable?"

"Your whole body tightens when I get close."

"Well, then, don't do that!" she fired back.

He looked at her with a smirk. "We're together, but we don't touch?"

Hannah heard him, but it sounded more complicated than what she had originally thought. Right now, she couldn't even tell what she had originally thought.

He reached out a hand and tucked a strand of hair behind her ear. The feel of his fingers tracing her ear made her lean in. A shiver went through her as he did it.

"It's casual touching between adults."

"So, you say."

"It says we spend time with each other."

"We do. We live in the same home, and there's no need for touching with our hands because our eyes work just fine."

"We've got to look natural."

"Natural what?"

He stepped closer to her again. This time she was prepared. "I'm not the enemy," he said as he lowered his forehead to hers.

"No, but you're not very obedient."

"It's because I lost my tail," he said with a grin. They just stood there head to head.

"Thank you. I know I can be difficult."

"You?"

"I don't know which one of us has a bigger problem. Me for asking or you for accepting."

"This won't be boring, Hannah. You might like being with me."

"Me? You're too rich and too pretty."

"Pretty is for girls."

"Ha! That says what you know. With those long horse lashes, you have, you know men can be pretty too."

They stayed head to head, just breathing for a minute, and then he spoke.

"Not bad, Padawan. Teach you I will."

Hannah heard the front door and thought it was Nathan. She was starting to pull away, but she knew he'd see them. Better to confront this part right now. Instead of hearing a shocked Nathan, she heard *his* voice.

All of her joy leeched out as if it were in a sieve. Her world tilted, and she waited to hear it again.

"What is going on here?"

Hannah looked at the door. Standing in what looked like torn up jeans and a dusty shirt was Henry Jenkins.

"Henry."

"Is that any way to greet the father of your child?"

Hannah closed her eyes. She just had to find a way not to kill him when she opened her eyes, and all would be well.

Nine

"What are you doing here?"

Henry stood in the doorway with a duffel bag at his feet. He was still a solidly built man. He had a little bit of a paunch in his middle, and his hair was starting to thin, but he wasn't bad to look at. On closer inspection, his shirt was wrinkled and had definitely seen better days.

Henry still dressed like he was in his twenties and hanging out in town. He was five foot eight, at best, and had, on first meeting, a little boy charm that pulled you in. Hannah could see all the things that had attracted her to him, but now she could see all the things he was missing as well.

He smiled and walked into the living room with his arms open. She didn't move. She used to tell him not to hug her, they weren't married. Then he would sulk about them having a life-long connection with Nathan. In the end, someone else always entered the room, and when they did, she looked like the bad guy not wanting to be civil.

This time he stopped in front of her, waiting. "No welcome for me, Hannah?"

"If you've come to see Nathan, yes, I welcome you, but I feel like this may be more than that, so I'll reserve judgment," she said stiffly.

"Hello, I'm Adam Cade." Hannah was jerked out of her fight mode with Henry. She looked over her shoulder and mouthed *sorry*. Adam just smiled, then he put his arm around her shoulder. Hannah didn't know who was more surprised—her or Henry—by the move.

"What do you want and why are you here?" Hannah asked.

"I came home to visit and see my son."

"You came with a duffel bag?"

Henry crossed his arms over his chest. It just accentuated how round his stomach was under the shirt. "You're not going to offer me water or an invitation to sit?"

Hannah wanted to say no. Nothing for you. Then she heard a noise behind him.

"Did you bring someone else with you?" she asked, gesturing to a man leaning in the doorway, looking trim and fit.

"Caleb is a friend who is traveling with me. He won't be a bother."

"Wow, if only I could say the same about you," Hannah groaned. "Take a seat and speak your peace."

Henry looked around and sat in the big chair opposite the couch. He and Nathan had picked it out as a fitting chair for Hannah. It was covered in knitted throws, as it had become her go-to place to knit.

"Is Nathan home?" Henry asked.

Hannah shook her head. "You're early. If you came for him, I'd call your sister because that's where he is."

Henry's eyes widened, and he shook his head. "I didn't know you still kept in touch with my sister."

Hannah laughed. "I didn't think it would matter to you one way or the other."

Henry shifted in the chair. "Hannah, I'm not the careless bad guy you make me out to be."

"We're not going there."

"Where is there? I'm just saying I'm trying to get my things together. We can't all be you," he said in a tight voice.

Hannah nodded. "Okay, let's not go over old territory. We know how this goes. You say I do everything. Then you accuse me of holding you to an impossible standard, and I get to be the perfectionist. This is old ground; why are we doing this?"

Hannah was grateful to feel the squeeze on her shoulder from Adam. Conversations with Henry never ended well, and they left her raw and guilty. Guilty that she couldn't make it work. Guilty that some part of her still blamed herself for giving up.

"Again, I have to ask, why are you here, Henry?"

Henry looked around the place and then focused back on her. "I think that I should be in Nathan's life more. I thought I could come home for a few days and make sure my son still knew me."

"Nathan knows who you are and what you are," Hannah replied. Then she hung her head, and Adam rubbed the tense muscles in her neck. "Listen, I'm sorry. I shouldn't have said that. You want time with Nathan, I'm all for it."

"I want to see if there is a place in his life for me. I want to be his father."

"I'm willing to try for Nathan, but Henry, be careful. He's my son, and I'll step in if I have to."

Henry stood up. "You think I'd do something to Nathan?"

Hannah let her shoulders slump, and the air went out of her. "No, Henry, I think you think about you first and believe that everyone else wants to do it the same way you do. You're not mean. You're just self-absorbed."

Henry sighed and looked like a lost soul. "I'm thinking I'll be at the Hotel. It's a bit more expensive than I thought."

Hannah heard the pitch for her to offer to let him stay at the house. She wouldn't do it. She knew it would probably make Nathan over the moon to have his dad in the house, but it cut too close to closed doors. She didn't want to give anyone any false hope.

"I'm sure they'll give you a discount. You're going to be there with your friend Caleb, and there isn't that much traffic this time of year."

"Fine, I'll give Nathan a call when I get settled," Henry said as he walked to the door.

"It's nice meeting you," Adam said. Hannah had almost forgotten he was there. He was so quiet.

After the door closed Adam said, "So that was Nathan's father."

Hannah knew her mouth was opening and closing like a fish out of water. Adam closed her mouth and kissed her on the forehead. "Don't worry. I told you I have your back. Get some rest. It seems like you just became a very popular and busy woman."

Hannah looked at Adam as he exited, wondering what he was talking about.

"I give up. What will be, will be."

"Henry? Is that you?" the hotel manager called out to Henry as he entered the front door. "It's me, Larry Cooper. I used to live down the way from you. Boy, it's sure strange to see you back here. I didn't know you'd be visiting. Why aren't you staying up at your place?"

Henry knew this would happen and he was dreading it. He would endure, though, because this visit wasn't about him; it was about Nathan.

"It's Hannah's place now, and I'm fine. I need a couple of rooms for the night."

"You know Clarissa has been saying that maybe Hannah should leave your ranch. I mean, the ranch has been in your family for a long time. It ain't right that a stranger should get it and be on the council as well."

Henry looked at Larry and wondered how often Hannah dealt with this. He didn't bother to answer the man because there would be no way to really answer it and get him to change his mind. At one time he would have tried to change his mind, but he understood that Larry just wanted to tear someone else down so he wouldn't think his life was so bad.

Being an adult was just as bad as he thought.

Henry made it to the room and looked out the window. He could see people moving about in Sweet Blooms. He knew that when Hannah looked at Sweet Blooms, she saw hope, a chance at a better life and possibilities. What he saw was a town that had defined him in terms of his father. A town that had judged him a good guy to work the land like his father before him. A town that couldn't see him at all.

He heard a noise and looked over his shoulder. It was Caleb. Caleb Matthews carried himself like a man who had seen so much that nothing shook him. He was a veteran of one of the branches. He was comfortable talking about life and death situations. Henry had even seen a weapon on Caleb once or twice. Caleb was the type of man who gave you a sense of peace if you knew he was on your side. The thing that stood out the most to Henry was that he was always looking. Always taking in his surroundings. Caleb was a dangerous man.

"Are you staying here long?"

He didn't know. Henry had met Caleb in the hospital. When he wasn't sure what the results would be, Caleb had been his counselor. When the scare was over, and Henry said he was going home, Caleb asked to tag along.

"I don't know why you're staying with me. I thought you'd leave as soon as we got here."

"Nope."

"Well, I don't need counseling. I know I'm here alone, and I know it's my fault. I don't need a counselor to tell me that." He went to sit at a little table in the room. On the table was a coffee maker and some water bottles.

"Why did you come back here, Henry?"

Henry looked at Caleb and then started the coffee maker. He knew he was stalling, just trying to find something to occupy his hands while he found the right answer. "I was in the hospital, and I realized I had no one to call. That if the tumor had been anything serious, no one would have cared."

"You have a son."

"In some ways, I do. He's mine. My name is on the birth certificate, but that's all I could claim. Did you see his mother, Hannah?"

"The attractive woman who looks like she's already in a relationship?" Caleb said.

"Yeah, it looks like I was too late for that too. Did you notice in the house there are no pictures of me? All of the pictures are of her and Nathan. I want my son to know me, and I want to know him. I want us to have photos and memories. I need to see if I can get that back."

Henry reached into his back pocket and pulled out a picture. He handed it to Caleb.

"This is all I have," he said.

Caleb took the picture.

Henry knew the picture like the back of his hand. It was the day he had come home with Nathan and Hannah from the hospital. He had made promises that day. Promises that he would be there for Hannah and Nathan. He had promised to be there to support Nathan like he hadn't been supported.

He couldn't remember when it all went south. He just remembered that when he was trying to do the things, he said he would, the ghosts of yesterday came back. Every day, while growing up in town, he would hear things like, "There's the Jenkins boy. He won't ever amount to anything. He doesn't do much at all."

"You all look like a family," Caleb said, handing the photo back to him.

Henry took it and folded it in half to go back in his wallet. "We were. I just couldn't hold on to it. Families are precious, Caleb. If you ever get one, do everything you can to keep it. It's too late for the family part, but I'm hoping it's not too late for my son and me." Henry looked at Caleb. "No words of advice? Do you even have kids, Caleb?"

"No kids. I don't stay around long enough for that. As for advice, every man has to walk a road made just for him. I would be out of place to give you advice about things I don't really know."

"You are so secretive, Caleb. What, are you wanted by several governments?"

"Nothing that special."

"We've been traveling together for a while, long enough for you to have some thoughts on me. Do you think I'm a good man?"

Caleb didn't say anything. He just looked at Henry and cocked his head to the side. "What are you looking for, Henry? At best, I'm a therapist, not a priest."

Henry laughed. "I'm not looking for absolution. I guess what I'm looking for is to understand how others see me when they meet me. I know what they used to think, but I've been away for a while, and you seem like a guy who would give it to me straight."

"I don't see the point in giving answers to questions you already know." With that, he left the room. Henry waited until the door was closed before he pulled out the picture again. Running his hand over Nathan's face, he brought it to his face and kissed the photo.

"I'm a good man, Nathan. I can be a good father."

Ten

"If you don't need a plate, we can share," Adam said. "I'll even get you some salad if you'd like."

Hannah watched Adam at the picnic. The other council members had definitely taken notice. Yesterday, after his grandmother had gone back to the city, Adam had agreed to this, and today they were sitting at a council picnic. She hadn't expected their show to start so soon. To say they were the talk of the town was an understatement.

Rarely did all the council members frequent these picnics, and even fewer town people ever showed up. The council actually created this impromptu event when there was an uptick in tourists. Hannah gave Adam her most piercing look. He was totally enjoying himself.

"Get whatever you think is appropriate, dear," she said through clenched teeth.

She had planned this to get everyone to accept her, but she didn't realize how under the microscope she'd feel. She'd already had more people than ever speak to her, by giving her a nod and sometimes a 'how are you.' Hannah was sure all the fawning would end when Clarissa showed up. That was the status quo. People could say hello when she was alone, but when Clarissa showed up, she became a pariah.

At first, people seemed confused about whether they could talk to Hannah, but when Adam sat next to her, several women smiled and said hello to them both. One or two of them seemed to be modeling instead of enjoying a nice picnic. Hannah tried not to gag at how obvious they were. Looking at Adam, a hint of doubt started to infect her thoughts. Adam was attractive. Maybe he was too attractive. She was glad that he didn't return any of the obvious invites while he was with her. In fact, if Hannah didn't know any better, she'd say he didn't even notice. He was courteous, brought back the plate of food, and sat with her as if she were the only one there.

As the hour went on, more women showed up to the event. You could tell some of them were just Lookie Lous. They had come by to see if it was true that Adam was with her. She looked at the plate Adam had brought and almost laughed out loud. It was full of carrots and celery sticks, with what looked like hummus, and some cut up pita wedges.

"There is no way we serve this," she said.

Adam smiled. "I asked a very nice man to get me some items from the store. For a tidy profit of three dollars, he was more than happy to oblige me."

Hannah looked at his innocent expression and laughed out loud. It was actually turning out to be a nice picnic. Until she heard Clarissa's voice.

As usual, she was wearing a dress that fit her as if it were made for her, with a vee that left little to the imagination. "Hello, Hannah. Please share what you find so amusing over there, hoarding Mr. Cade to yourself."

It was the same every time they met. This had been going on for so long that Hannah didn't even blink at Clarissa's innuendo and rudeness. What she really wanted to see was how Adam would react. Hannah plastered on the same disinterested smile she always had for Clarissa.

Sweet Blooms was a great place to live, but it had a bad apple. She just so happened to be on the board and looked like she'd just stepped off a magazine cover. While there was no denying Clarissa was beautiful on the outside, the rest of her nature seemed dark as could be. She seemed to have a thing for making Hannah's life consistently bad.

"I don't mind being hoarded by a beautiful woman," Adam replied. Even Hannah had to turn towards him. She wanted to stand up and pump her arm in the air and say, "In your face, he thinks I'm beautiful!"

After Hannah got her five-year-old self in check, she turned back toward Clarissa.

"I assure you I'm not hoarding. Adam is free to make his own decisions." Then Hannah picked up a carrot from the shared plate and dipped it into the hummus.

"Adam invited me out since we see each other every day at my home. He thought I would be the perfect person to show him around town. That way he can see other businesses and try to come up with some ways to help the town. I had no choice but to say yes. You know you've been trying for months, and I think Adam may have some new ideas to help us."

Hannah didn't know how it was possible, but it seemed like everyone on the lawn had stopped and was listening to the conversation.

"Well, I can see that Adam is bringing out a whole new side of you," Clarissa quipped.

"Maybe you're right. Maybe that's what I needed—a new chance and someone with whom to fill up my afternoons."

Clarissa turned, so she was facing Adam and not Hannah.

"If you need to see the other parts of town, let me know. I'll be glad to show you on behalf of the council." She smiled and nodded at Adam and then walked off. When Clarissa looked over her shoulder, she found a group of people looking startled and turned to look at something else.

Hannah had known the first meeting would be tense. All of the tightness in her body fell away when she heard a loud crunch next to her. As if nothing had happened, Adam was eating away at his carrots.

"These carrots really were a good idea," he said.

A group of people approached and asked him where he had gotten them, and he referred him to the boy who had fetched them. Some of them left to find the boy, but others who were braver sat around and engaged them both in conversation. Hannah wasn't thrilled with the way this had started, but she was happy and surprised by how soon people included her in the conversation.

An hour later, the picnic was wrapping up. Adam made sure to take a walk with her around the picnic under the premise of seeing what food had been provided.

"That wasn't so bad," Adam said as he walked hand in hand with her back to their original seats.

She looked up at him and thought she would see a sarcastic face. Instead, she saw he was serious.

"Thank you," she said.

Adam cocked his head to the side and smiled. "Did you enjoy it?"

She wanted to say that maybe *enjoy* wasn't the right word. It was like the school nerd getting the jock on prom day. To boot, people were just about gone, and Adam was still holding her hand in his, and was resting it on his thigh. She never realized how muscular thighs could be. Even covered in his go-to jeans, being this close to him was a distraction.

"Hannah?"

She pulled her gaze up to his face and remembered he was asking her a question. Did she enjoy herself?

"You were great the way you did the rounds and made nice to everyone."

"How do you know I'm not naturally nice?" he joked.

Her gaze fell back to their joined hands.

"You could have given Clarissa some more attention. I know she's beautiful, and no one would have held it against you."

"We're going to have to work on that, Hannah."

"Work on what?"

"That self-esteem issue. If I'm out with a woman, no other woman exists for me. They can offer, but I don't have to take."

Hannah peered up at his face.

"Maybe," she said softly.

"Maybe what?" he asked, confused.

"I'm not sure if you're a nice guy, but I know you are an attractive one. So, we'll wait and see."

"So, you find me attractive?" he said as he lifted her hand to his mouth.

She yanked her hand from his. "Don't fish for

compliments. You know you're attractive. And what does that mean—when you're with a woman, no other exists? Are you interested in someone already? If you saw someone at the picnic or when you dropped off your grandmother, and you want to be with them—"

"Hold up—" he said, interrupting her. He stood up and faced her. Sitting on the bench, she realized he was really tall. He also made her feel petite. She couldn't remember a time when someone had made her feel that way. It was strange, but with him standing in front of her, for the first time in a while, she felt safe.

"I'm not interested in anyone," he said. "When I said I concentrate on one woman at a time, I was talking about you."

"Me? Oh, well, I guess that's okay considering what we're trying to do and all."

If it were possible, Adam took a step closer to her. "I thought we could go out to dinner sometime. What's your thought?"

"Dinner? You don't like my cooking?"

Adam laughed. "I love your cooking. I thought you might want a break. Plus, you'll be cooking more when Nathan comes home."

Nodding, she looked at him and shrugged. "I don't really know a place for dinner that everyone would talk about. I mean we could—"

"Hannah, I want to spend time with you."

"I know. I'm saying we should do it where everyone can see us and—"

Adam reached out and trailed a fingertip across her cheek. His finger left tingles everywhere he touched.

"I don't care who sees us. I want to spend time with you alone. To get to know you."

Hannah looked around; the park was about empty, and no one was there. "You know me already. You see me at mealtime."

"I've never seen you when you go to dinner."

"It's not fancy. I'll put on a regular dress and put my hair in a bun. I'm not what they call classically beautiful."

"You look beautiful, and I'd like to get to know Hannah, the woman." Hannah heard the words coming out of his mouth, and she wanted to believe him. Out of all the people on the planet, he should know about good-looking women since he had dated one of the most beautiful women in the world.

"I don't get you. I thought we agreed on what we were doing," she said, frustrated. "I thought we were going to go around and you would help me become more involved with the town."

"This is definitely about involvement."

"There's no one here! We are practically alone in the park. If we went to dinner, it would be the same thing."

"Involvement isn't something that just happens in public. If we don't work on being comfortable with each other, then when we are in public, it will look fake and contrived."

Hannah let out a deep breath and tried to think. Who could think clearly with Adam standing in front of them? "Why can't we just stick to a public script and leave it at that?"

"Because the reason you are in this mess is that they don't know you."

Hannah considered what he said and realized this plan was spiraling out of control. "I don't know if I agree with getting to know me, but I'll try. I'm warning you. I'm not good at this."

He smiled at her. "This?"

She waved her hands around. "You know, this! The getting to know people section."

He put his hand under her chin and then leaned down and placed a kiss on her lips. It wasn't invasive or demanding. It was soft and sweet. "Don't worry, I've got you. See you tonight for dinner."

With that, he turned and walked away. Hannah was standing there looking at him as if he were some hero off to war. Oh yeah, she thought, this was definitely more than what she had bargained for.

Eleven

Henry wanted to see Nathan. He figured the best place would be on the football field. The last time they had talked, Nathan had told him he enjoyed playing football. He knew where they were going to be practicing. It was the same place he had practiced at Sweet Blooms High. Sitting in the car, he saw the guys running into one another.

He stood beside the rental truck that Caleb had insisted on. He saw parents, mostly fathers in the bleachers, rooting for their sons.

"Maybe I should have asked Hannah," he muttered.

Caleb was next to him in blue jeans and a dark blue shirt. "Maybe, could have, would have. That's all done with now because we're here."

"Is the world really that black and white to you?" he asked.

"When I see you and your family, yes. When it's my own…not so much."

Henry took a look at Caleb, hoping to see some sort of expression on his face. When it was apparent nothing was going to make him change his facial expression, he turned back to the field and took a big breath.

"Okay, I'm going to meet my son."

He walked around the fence toward the opening and tried to catch sight of Nathan. He looked for a boy small in stature, or for a jersey that said 'Jenkins' on it. When none of them seemed to jump out to him, he made a beeline to the coach on the sideline. The coach looked young, lean, and not like anybody he knew in Sweet Blooms.

"Can I help you?"

"I'm passing through, and I saw this game and wondered if you could tell me what position Jenkins is playing."

The coach gave him the once over and then shrugged. "You've got the wrong team. There's no Jenkins here."

Henry absorbed the shock internally. "Is this the only team? Do you have a junior team or—"

The coach shook his head. "You must be from outside. Sweet Blooms only has one team. We put all the different ages together in the warm-up. If you look on the field now, everyone who is on the team is out there. When we get ready to practice, we separate the younger ones and those who are on the bench or serving as backups on the bleachers."

Henry nodded and started toward the fence. He saw Caleb standing by the truck. He stopped midway and looked back at the field. He remembered the last time he was with Nathan, how he had bragged about him making the team. Right after he said it, he had asked him if he would come to Sweet Blooms to visit. At the time he had said no, he was working. Now Henry wondered what else Nathan had said that wasn't true. Why would he lie to him?

When Henry finally made it to Caleb, he stopped in front of him.

"He's not on the team?" Caleb asked. "Boys like to impress their fathers."

Henry didn't say anything; instead, he just leaned against the truck. "Impress me? He had to know I'd find out." He looked to Caleb who had that blank expression on his face again. Henry cleared his throat and nodded.

"Or maybe he thought I'd never find out because he never expected me to actually show up." Henry pushed away from the truck and started to walk away. "I'll see you at the hotel later."

"Where are you going, Henry?"

"Walking. I need to clear my head, and I need to be alone."

Henry didn't know where he was going. Where could he go? He wanted to make a change. He wanted to be a part of Nathan's life. Hannah had moved on, and it looked like he had already lost Nathan.

Growing up, he had always been a Jenkins. The Jenkins family wasn't known for much, but he was determined to be different. He wanted a wife everyone envied, so he had dated Clarissa, the town beauty queen. That hadn't lasted.

Then he had left Sweet Blooms to make a name for himself and instead wound up getting married to Hannah and having Nathan. Hannah was the one who always encouraged him, but when they came back, the past came back, and he was once again just a Jenkins.

When he thought they should go back, she'd said no, that Sweet Blooms was best for Nathan. He left, thinking for sure she would follow him. He should've known better. Hannah was a force to be reckoned with.

There was nothing she wouldn't do for Nathan, and that included divorcing him.

He found himself in front of Banter House. He walked in and took a booth. A few minutes later, Caleb walked in and sat down in the booth opposite him.

"I thought you were going back to the hotel," said Henry.

"I get hungry too," Caleb answered.

A waitress in sandaled feet came over with the menus. "Oh, lookie, you're Nathan's dad," she said.

Henry looked up at her, trying to decide if he knew her.

"No, you don't know me," the waitress said, "but Nathan has shown me your picture."

"You know Nathan?"

"Yes, I just said I did. I'm Geeta. What do you want to eat?"

Henry was at a loss for words, so Caleb jumped in and ordered.

"Two bacon burgers deluxe if you have them."

Geeta looked Caleb over. "It must be the advertising. Now we have a regular trail of men who are easy on the eyes coming to town."

Geeta left, and Henry leaned on the table. "She knows Nathan. I wonder what she knows."

"Have you considered asking her?" Caleb replied.

Henry shook his head. "I don't think so. I—"

Caleb already had his hand up, and Geeta came by.

"You forget something?"

Caleb shook his head. "No. We just wanted to know how well you know Nathan."

Geeta looked at Henry and tsked. "Why are you here in town?"

Henry looked from Caleb to Geeta before answering. "I came to be with Nathan and—"

"So, you didn't want the boy, and now you do?"

"No, I want him. I was just confused."

Geeta gave him a long look for a minute and then let out a sigh. "I shouldn't give you a hard time. I like Nathan. He helps me in the kitchen. The boy can cook," she said with a smile.

Henry smiled at Caleb. "Did you hear? My boy can cook."

"I'm right here, so yes, I did."

Geeta laughed at that response. She faced Henry. "You might be ready for Nathan if you've come here."

"I know a lot of people may not think I'm ready, but I've grown up. I've had some hardships, but what matters is my son."

Another waitress brought the burgers out and placed them in front of them both. She hung around for a moment and smiled at Caleb. When Geeta noticed, she quickly addressed the girl.

"You think I'm paying you to ogle customers that look like eye candy? No, I'm sure there are some things to be done."

Geeta harrumphed and then turned her focus back on Henry. "I've been here a minute, so let me give you some advice. Wait for Nathan to be as ready as you are."

Henry was shocked. "Ready? Of course, Nathan is ready. He's my son."

Geeta threw up her hands. "I knew it was a bad idea to try and tell a goat anything, but I tried. I'll be here if you need me."

"I just need my son. He needs me," Henry said with conviction.

Geeta walked away and threw over her shoulder, "Let me know how that goes, because we all may think we're open to accept what we need when it comes, but that's not always true."

Twelve

Hannah was finishing up her last class for the day. It was an advanced design class and she only had four students, all in high school. It was a joy to see how her students created new designs in her arts and crafts class that they would teach next semester.

As they were leaving the class, Eve's dad stopped to talk. Hannah knew this would have never happened pre-Adam. She was curious to hear what he wanted to talk about.

"Hello, Hannah. I wanted to tell you there was a guy around the field today asking what position Jenkins played. I didn't think about it until I got here. Be careful and tell Nathan too. As we get bigger, we have to look out for our own."

Hannah nodded and waited for him to leave. She knew who the stranger was. At the same time, she was angry with Henry for going to the school, and she was heartbroken at the thought Nathan had lied to Henry. She was heartbroken that he felt the need to and helpless to do anything about it.

The Director came smiling around the corner. "It looks like you have someone to give you a ride home."

Hannah braced herself to see Henry. She was sure he wanted to talk about Nathan and why he wasn't playing football. Instead, when she went outside, Adam was waiting for her. He was leaning against the car looking like a model straight off a billboard.

Even when he was standing still, he was still working a room. He had long, lean lines that begged for a woman to run her hands along them. The package was impressive all together, but she was still partial to his hands. After the picnic, she was willing to entertain the fact that his lips deserved some credit too. The man could kiss. While she reminisced over the previous kiss, a nagging thought started to form in her mind. Would he kiss her when it was just them? Were all the kisses just for show? Would he ever kiss her because he wanted to kiss her?

"Hello pretty lady," he said.

"You do know that there aren't really a lot of people around the center."

"You never know where busybodies might show up. The coast looks clear, and then you kiss one girl, and they pop out of the bushes. Yesterday, an innocent peck on the cheek becomes a passionate embrace today."

She smiled at him. "Ah, yes, I had totally forgotten about them. They must be right up there with the grannies who hang out the window all day and all night long so they can give the authorities the exact times of your comings and goings."

Adam snapped his fingers and pointed at her. "You do understand!"

Laughing with him, she looked around him. He looked behind himself as well.

"You're looking for…?"

"I wanted to make sure Henry wasn't here."

"The guy we met the other night? I thought he was visiting Nathan."

"I think that's part of the problem. He didn't tell Nathan, and I think Nathan has embellished some things to impress his father."

"Ouch! I know father-son relationships can be problematic."

Hannah's smile fell away. "It's a work in progress. I don't know why Henry just showed up now. It almost seems like he's ready to be a dad to Nathan. I can't imagine that without an act of God."

Adam was listening to her, and she was complaining away. Hannah wasn't sure why she was so comfortable with Adam. It wasn't the kisses or the pretense that they were together. Adam gave feedback and seemed like he really wanted to hear what she had to say.

There was also the fact that he was treating her like she was his. She had an idea of what that might entail, but he had blown every thought she had out of the water. Being his meant she never knew what to expect. It was exciting and scary all at the same time.

"Earth to Hannah," Adam said, tapping her on the shoulder. "If you have that look in your eyes, people will think I'm so boring that you randomly space out to escape me."

"Really?"

"Hey, at least three busybodies jumped out of the bushes and shook their heads for the day."

"Okay, I admit I was distracted, but three busybodies?" she said incredulously.

"Well, I wanted to come by and talk about doing this in a more controlled way."

"Doing what?"

"Our being together."

"Oh!" She didn't know why, but she was feeling wary after hearing his words. A schedule? Who would have thought about a schedule? Well, she could just throw away any of those silly notions of him being interested in doing anything with her outside of their deal.

"So, I'm thinking we should be regularly dating."

She heard the words come out of his mouth and still couldn't put them together in her head. "Dating? What do you mean dating?"

He reached out and pulled her into his arms. "I'm talking about me and you going out together. Sometimes we'd eat. Sometimes we'd walk around and make moon eyes at each other. Sometimes we'd just be with each other for no reason other than we like to be around each other. You know, dating."

That would be dangerous, Hannah wasn't sure she'd be able to keep her growing feelings for him in check if they spent that much time together. "Or we can just show up in places at the same time and seem really interested in each other."

He grinned. "Nah, we couldn't do that. It's so passé. The ages of randomly meeting are over. Technology and all. While I thank you for the input, I think when you really think it over, you'll agree that my way is the better way. Let's date!"

She glanced behind her. No one was close to them on the street. "Keep your voice down and let's go somewhere else to talk about this."

He let her go and moved to open his car door. "I'm glad we had this discussion. I want to start dating as soon as possible. I won't be home tonight as I'm working on my house. I'll see you here tomorrow, and we can talk and date then."

She wanted to argue with him. She wanted to strangle him. She didn't do either because he got in his car and went away. Date? He wanted to date. Nope, it was totally unnecessary. When she was finished with him, he'd understand. Tonight, she had to take care of her son and her ex's unexpected return.

Nathan was her pride and joy. She wanted the best for him, and she was willing to make sacrifices to make sure that happened. Her own childhood wasn't memorable or pleasant. She needed to make sure Nathan had the completely opposite experience. She was trying to get the whole notion of dating out of her head when she heard Nathan come in the front door.

"Nathan?"

He didn't answer. Hannah knew this wasn't boding well at all. She left the kitchen and saw him by the front door.

"Nathan?"

When he turned toward her, she could see the distress in his face. She did what she had been doing since he was born—she opened her arms, and he ran into them. She didn't ask him any questions; she just held him. When his grip had lightened, she walked him over to the couch. She pulled him into her embrace again.

"So, I take it you know your father is in town?" she started. He nodded against her side.

"Are you planning on seeing him?" Nathan shook his head against her side.

"Nathan, it's very hard to have a conversation with a person who will only talk into the side of your body."

He pulled away and looked at her. It broke her heart to see her little boy like this.

"Tell me what I can do," she said in a soft voice.

Nathan wiped his face, sniffed, and then took a deep breath.

"Make him go away."

"Nathan—"

"Mom, you don't understand."

"Nathan, your father—"

"He never should have come!"

"Nathan, I need you to get yourself together and stop saying that." Nathan hung his head, and Hannah could feel the tears falling from his face.

She pulled him back into her arms. "Nathan, baby, please help me understand. It's always been us two, don't shut me out now."

"I was just getting the guys to like me, and now he's here," Nathan mumbled.

"Why does it matter?"

"Because I told them the reason, he didn't come was that he was working in the city doing something important. Now he's here, and they are going to know. They're going to know and—"

Hannah tilted his chin back. "Why, Nathan?"

The tears continued to fall down his cheeks until they were pooling beneath his chin.

"I had to. They would all talk about their dads, and I wanted to be able to say something. Anything! They were talking about how they went on trips and how they went places with their dads, and I couldn't say anything."

"We do things, Nathan. I know it's not your dad but—"

"But what, mom? I'm supposed to tell the guys that I went camping with my mom the year I graduated from sixth grade?"

"We did!"

"I can't say that to them. They all had dads that were doing things, so when I talked about doing things that we did together, I just told them that dad took me instead," he said in a small voice. Hannah nodded and wiped the tears from his face.

She was dying inside. She had to remember this was about Nathan. Not about how she had studied for those trips and taken him so he wouldn't miss those "boy events." Funny that she didn't know she had just been a stand-in for Henry.

"Mom, I'm sorry."

She looked at him for a moment, as he waited for her to respond.

"So, I'm not thrilled that I was your dad's stand-in, but I understand. I'm sorry, Nathan. I didn't know you felt this way or that you felt you had to do this. I wish I had known."

"You know how we say it's just us two all the time. Now he's back and he'll ruin everything when they ask him about stuff, and he says he's never been there. I just want to be a part of the guys, and I feel like I finally am one of them. Now he's here." He sniffled into the back of his hand. "He doesn't come when he says, and when he does come, I have to bring money for us both—"

"Nathan, I told you, your dad pays child support and it—"

"Mom, Lyle's mom works in the courthouse, and he doesn't like me. He told me dad doesn't pay anything."

"Nathan, your dad isn't perfect, but he does pay sometimes. Don't think the worst about him. Without him, I wouldn't have you. I never want you to not be able to talk to your father."

Nathan sat up and wiped his face. "Is he staying?"

"I don't know, honey. I'll try to find out, and I'll talk to him. In the meantime, I want you to be open-minded. I want you to get to know him if you can. I think family is very important. We all do things for different reasons. Can you do that?"

Nathan smiled. "I can try." He held out his hand "We're in this together?"

Hannah saw his hand and placed hers on top. "We're in this together."

Then she reached out and hugged him close. "Okay, off to your room to get your studies done. It's late, so no cooking tonight."

Nathan peered up at her and wiggled his eyebrows. "What if I told you I had an amazing recipe for chocolate cupcakes?"

"No way, buddy! Off to your room."

"Okay."

Hannah watched him go upstairs and then grabbed the pillow on the couch and held it close. She let the tears fall. She just hoped she could talk to Henry and they could do the best thing for their son.

Thirteen

Adam had a plan. He and Hannah would be the only ones in the house tonight. He knew she wasn't keen on the idea of dating, but he was. Adam had stopped by the nursery and bought her a flat of seedlings of herbs. It wasn't flowering in the traditional sense, but it would fit Hannah perfectly.

When he heard her pulling into the driveway, he went to the door to meet her. He could see her carrying a basket of knitting and materials. He thought about going to help her, but he knew if he went outside to do it, she would take it wrong. Hannah was very independent. She wasn't walking with her regular pep. He wondered if today's classes had been more challenging than normal.

She was wearing another shapeless skirt and top. Adam wondered if she just dropped something over the top of her head and kept going. Her black hair was in a ponytail, and her bare face had a couple freckles that he thought were sexy and made her look like a real woman. What he did notice about all of the skirts she wore was that they all had pockets. He wondered if the skirts were a product of her working at the center and needing to put things from her knitting class in those pockets.

When she got to the door, and he opened it, she paused. "Oh, you're here."

"I am. I wanted to start this off right, so I brought a gift." He reached behind himself and got the flat of seedlings.

Hannah smiled. "I can see you are putting real effort into this."

"I don't mind working for what I want."

"Humph." What could she say? "You're going to have to take these back, as much as I adore them."

"They're seedlings. Hannah."

Hannah traced her hands over the delicate seedlings. She thought about where she could plant them and how much space they'd need, and then she stopped herself.

"The problem is, Adam, I'm not going to date you. We had an agreement and—"

"And I'm changing it."

She looked at him incredulously. "No. You can't. Why are you doing this?"

He took her basket and then walked her over to the couch. "Hannah, it occurred to me that I might really like you."

"Like me?" she repeated.

"Do you have a reason you can't date me?"

"Yes."

Adam waited and then smiled. "The way this normally works is when someone has a problem, they say what it is. Why do you not want to date me?"

"Because you're perfect."

Adam stopped. "Excuse me?"

"Listen, Adam, I think you're a nice guy."

"But—"

"But I already said it. You're perfect. You look good. You've got all your teeth. Good hair."

"Am I a guy or a horse?"

Hannah held up her hands. "Listen, don't take offense, but I'd be lying to you if I told you I hadn't looked at your outside first. You're incredibly good looking. You have money, and you want to settle down. What man does that?"

Adam was confused. "And—"

"And I'm not any of those things. I'm a regular woman. I make enough money so my kid and I can be comfy. I want to settle down, but I've got a child. Listen, I can't talk about it. We just can't do it."

She tried to leave the couch, but he reached out for her hands.

"I think you're beautiful."

"Adam—"

"I think you're amazing with the house, and with the knitting online and off. I think Nathan is great too. You and he have a close relationship, and there is a lot of trust between you two, so he can go off and still be a guy and not be worried that you're going to care for him differently."

"I've seen you in a tee shirt. You've got a six pack."

"It's true, but it'll go away. I had a gym to go to every day. I'm doing work, but it's not the same, and I can tell you I can feel that six pack slipping away."

"Adam…"

"What's really bothering you, Hannah?"

"It's me."

"You said that, but there's nothing wrong with you."

"I pick men that all seem good, but then they have

some horrible trait that I don't find out until later, and it's usually something that was staring me in the eye."

"So, you're saying you know I have a problem and I just haven't told you?"

"Something like that."

"We'll just have to go over this. First, I like you as is, Hannah. Second, you are a pain sometimes, but I like you. And third, my problem is I have money, but no one can see me for me."

Hannah looked at their hands clasped together. "I'm scared to make another mistake like that. It's not just me, it's Nathan too."

"Give me a chance, Hannah," he murmured in a soft tone.

Hannah looked at their hands for a few more moments and then squeezed his. "What kind of seedlings did you get me?"

He grinned. "Mint, hops, basil, and others."

"Then based on the good foundation of herbs I need in my garden, let's give it a shot."

She went to the flat, and both of them went to the garden. It was like an old habit now. She picked up her gardening kit while he picked up the knee pads. Both of them made it to the garden and took up their positions in their respective rows.

He could see the cleared spaces. He waited for her to hand out the seedlings for him to put in his row.

"I've been meaning to get something. These bare patches drive me crazy." She handed out his share of plants and both of them got to work.

Hannah began to hum as she was planting. Adam stared at her, knowing she had no idea how adorable she looked. This was Hannah, pure and simple. She didn't have a fake smile, and she wasn't trying to impress anyone. She was just Hannah. Every day he realized what a treasure she was.

He picked up a seedling and began to plant it in his rows. "About our dating," he said as he opened up the ground. "I'd like to pick the places."

"Wow, you're going to talk about that while we're in the garden?"

"I think it's a great time. You're doing something you enjoy, and I'm talking about something I enjoy."

"I think that's your work side coming out. Doing all that multi-tasking."

Adam grinned. "I think it's safe to say that people do things they both enjoy at the same time. Sometimes they even enjoy the same thing but for different reasons. Like us being out here in the garden. You like gardening. I like being with you."

Hannah looked up and swallowed. "You are messing with my head."

"You think I don't like being with you?" He could see the wary expression on her face.

"I didn't say that. I'm saying I'm pretty ordinary, and I think you're not bothered by me, is all."

"You have a lot of thoughts about what I think," he said with a smile.

"It's not hard. It's common sense."

He reached out and tucked an errant strand of hair behind her ear. He felt the shudder of awareness go through her, and he smiled. "Common sense isn't so common from what I hear."

"This isn't dating," she said in a whisper.

"It's part of the process. It's called the sweet beginnings."

"I should go inside now."

"I have another idea," he said, leaning across the row, careful not to crush any of the seedlings.

"What would that be?" she asked in a small voice.

"How about, to seal the deal, I kiss you," he said.

"You don't have to. I'll take your word."

"You could, but why risk it?" He leaned in and brushed his mouth against hers. Just when he felt her respond, he pulled back and then pressed his mouth to her cheek. He placed a trail of light kisses across her cheek until he was at her ear, and then he kissed her right behind her ear before taking a small nibble from her earlobe. When he pulled back, he saw her flushed cheeks and parted lips. Then her eyes opened. He saw her tongue come out and lick her bottom lip.

"And that was?" she asked.

"Sweet beginnings," he said.

Before he could say anything else, they were interrupted by the closing of the front door.

"Mom!" Nathan called.

Adam stood up and brushed off his jeans. "See you soon, Hannah." He had to walk away. She had no idea the effect she had on him and until recently, he hadn't understood it. He was a businessman. He understood you had to grab an opportunity when it appeared, but plans changed sometimes. He could see the plan needed to be amending between Hannah and him.

Fourteen

Here she was, driving to the home of the man who said they would be dating. She knew their dating was for the crowds, but it was dating, nonetheless. She didn't know why she was nervous. She'd been out to this plot of land before Adam had bought it.

If she were honest, it had nothing to do with the land and everything to do with the man. He made her feel like a woman again. She had to remember that this wasn't real. What had she heard in town? Hannah didn't want to "catch feelings" in this. When she had originally thought of the plan, she thought she would be able to keep her distance. That had officially gone out the window.

If she wasn't sure just how out of her depth she was, the feeling in the pit of her stomach was reminder enough. Here she was with butterflies in her stomach. She wasn't even sure what excuse she was going to give as to why she had come out here. She got out of the truck and walked with all of the authority she could muster but didn't feel.

She walked up to the door and considered ringing the bell but let that option pass as she saw the cracked door.

She could hear his voice floating out the door to the porch. As she walked in, what she thought should have been the living room was just a large room with no furniture in it. Again, she heard the voices and recognized one of them to be Adam.

Hannah heard the voices rise again in the other room.

"They'll be in there all day."

Hannah turned and saw a woman coming down the steps with a suitcase. She was about five-five, with a black pixie cut and a lean body. "It's my brother and the accountant. They'll be at it all day."

"What is the possibility that they would both listen to a third option that says hire it out?"

The young lady laughed and shook her head. "That was Luke's position."

Holding out her hand, Hannah said, "Sorry. I'm Hannah Jenkins, and you are?"

"I'm Chance Cade, but everyone calls me CeeCee. I've got to make a flight. Since Adam is out here, I run the day to day operations."

Hannah smiled at the woman. "Is this the norm?"

"Well, ever since Adam decided to come out here, his accountant Luke, has had to come out here as well. The problem, of course, being Luke doesn't like anything that's not the city. They're arguing over numbers. Luke wants to do it for the cheapest amount. Adam just wants to haggle."

Hannah realized she hadn't really asked Adam about his business or how the transition was going. She remembered him saying his sister would take over. "What number are they fighting over?"

"They're fighting over the amount it will take to

finish the house and add the woodworking building he wants to put on the side."

"I didn't know he was going to build it out here. I thought he was going to be at the center."

CeeCee reached the bottom of the steps and then extended the handle on her luggage to pull it behind her.

"He will, he just wants to do some apprenticing. For that, he needs a shop. He's leaving the business, but he's not leaving what he enjoys. He's leaving the barracudas and lawyers to me," she said with a smile.

"You don't look upset over it," Hannah commented.

CeeCee's smile widened. "That's my fun. Besides, I love when they see me and think it's going to be so easy to make the deal. Then they find out I've got bigger teeth."

CeeCee and Hannah laughed. Hannah looked over her shoulder but couldn't hear the conversation slowing down at all.

"Why don't I take you to the airport? It doesn't look like they're letting up anytime soon."

CeeCee rolled her eyes. "Thanks, I'd appreciate it. If I stopped Luke now, he'd be talking about how right he is during the car ride."

"Great, let's go."

Hannah would have to ask Adam about his plans later, but it was too tempting to talk to someone else who knew Adam.

Adam had been going over the plans and the numbers all morning with Luke, his best friend and company accountant. They had at least gotten the budget under control. The issue was how many people he would have to bring in without disturbing the town. He didn't want the town to lose what made it Sweet Blooms just because he needed an apprentice workshop.

He went to the only habitable room in the house. It was set up as a breakroom/kitchen. Luke was there getting himself another cup of coffee. Luke and Adam had met each other when they were both starting out. Luke was the best accountant there was in the corporate world. He loved the city and didn't really understand what Adam was doing coming back to this town. The only reason he had supported it was because he could see the profit in the move for Adam.

"You know, if you had stayed at the place I'm staying, we could have hashed this out in a day or so." Adam said as he made his way to the coffee machine.

"Humph, I dare not. I'm at a hotel," Luke told him.

"You scared, Luke?" Adam teased.

"I've seen the googly eyes you have. Whatever is happening at the bed and breakfast you're at, I don't want it."

"You might like this life if you gave it a chance," Adam said.

Luke faced him. "The town lacks some necessities."

"Like?"

"Noise, police sirens, and a Starbucks on every other corner." He ticked off his fingers.

Adam held up his hands. "You're right. It turns out those were pluses for me."

Luke grinned. "That's what happens when you make it to a big office with a window. You get bored."

"It's cleaner here than in New York," Adam said.

"It's probably cleaner in Heaven, but I don't plan on going there to find out."

"You're sending Katherine to finish up?" Adam asked.

"Katherine has been odd lately. She's a talented woman, but I think she needs a break, and this is as close as I can get to tell her to take a vacation."

Adam knew Luke collected talented people who didn't quite fit in anywhere else. You wouldn't know he had a heart of gold. Luke lived in suits. The joke was that he went to bed in a suit and had been born in a suit and would probably be found dead in a suit while buying a suit. His blond hair and blue eyes gave people the wrong impression that he was easy-going and friendly. In reality he was all business all the time. His schedule was packed because he was in high demand.

"So, we've been going over these numbers, and I'm going to need someone to be my project overseer."

Luke nodded. "True. The day-to-day needs to be managed, as do the contracts. If you don't want to do that, you need to get someone who can."

"I'm trying to decide between hiring local or bringing someone from the city. Normally this wouldn't be a problem. I'd just go over the last project and then pick from the end results. This is a smaller town. I want to preserve the town and not have it flooded with people from the outside. I can, of course, tell them my requirements, but I wonder if it would be better if I just started with someone from the town."

"Have you seen anyone in the town who can even do this?"

"I have. He's a bit eccentric. He's on the council, but everyone says that he's a good man for this. He's older, but I have to tell you I've heard nothing but good things about him. I've spoken to him a couple of times and he's direct, but he's never left this town. This project might be bigger than him."

"And what's your other option?"

"I'd go to the agency for one of the guys who built Cade Designs in the city. He would know what I'm doing conceptually." Adam put his coffee cup down. "I like Jerry. He's got the character, and this forthrightness is a good fit for where I am right now."

"It seems like you know what you should do."

Adam looked at Luke. "This is important, man. It's not just for me. It's for my future family."

Luke patted him on the back. "It seems like it's true that things happen in cycles. We were in this same position before when you were starting Cade Designs after your father passed away. Follow your instincts and what feels right. That's why you came here, right? You had a feeling?"

"I guess." With that, Luke left, and Adam was still pondering what to do. He thought about Sweet Blooms and wanting to make sure everything was perfect. He knew everyone was looking at him and he didn't want to fail in front of everyone. He left the break room and went to his truck to get the city number.

Henry stepped out of his truck and then walked down the road to a small pond. He had agreed to meet Nathan here. It was the pond he had taught him to fish at. He was surprised that he wanted to meet here at all. Henry was ready to take him to a nice restaurant and buy him some clothes if he wanted. He walked to the clearing and saw Nathan sitting on the grass by the pond.

"Nathan?"

Nathan turned to face him and stood up. He had a tentative smile on his face.

"I'm surprised you wanted to meet here," he said.

"I thought it would be the best place. We've had fun here, and we both know how to get here."

Henry looked around, and it dawned on him. This place was totally secluded. No one would see them here together. Talking with Hannah wasn't going well, so he had decided to reach out to Nathan on his cell and ask if they could get together. He was sure the problem was Hannah. He was hoping that Hannah was the problem. After the football incident, he just wasn't sure.

"Let's sit over there; mom packed a lunch for us."

"You didn't have to bother your mother."

Nathan laughed. "It's not a bother. She loves doing these for me. When I was smaller, she would pack my lunch and put all kinds of smiling faces in it. Now when I say I want lunch, she always asks me if she can put "art" in it. Today I told her yes, so I don't know what kind of kiddie things will be in it."

Henry followed him to the blanket he hadn't been able to see before. They sat on the blanket and handed out the food. True to Nathan's words, there was art in the basket. Chicken nuggets in the shape of stars. Jell-O in the shape of small animals and finger sandwiches cut into shapes.

Henry laughed. "You were right. She really does like food art."

"When she started buying me food molds for things I wanted to make, she started using them as well. I think she has more fun with it."

Henry looked at Nathan, who was smiling and relaxed. He popped a nugget in his mouth.

"I didn't know you liked to cook."

Nathan stopped and looked at him before looking away.

"I've been doing it since I was nine or ten."

"I take it you haven't been doing football."

Nathan took a deep breath and then looked up at Henry. "I'm small. I don't do football because I'm too small and I can't catch or throw the ball right."

Henry looked confused. "You can't throw? Throwing isn't that hard. I can show you."

"No." Nathan looked away, and Henry could see the tension taking over his body. His shoulders were tense, and he began to fidget. "I'm sorry. I didn't mean to say it like that, but I don't want to play football anymore. Mom tried to teach me how to throw back in the day."

"Ouch! Your mother can't throw to save her life. It was always funny to me she could read patterns and do all the complex stuff with her knitting, but a ball she just never got the hang of."

"Well, I never got the hang of it either," Nathan said in a small voice.

Henry reached across the food to touch Nathan's shoulder, and Nathan backed away. He let his hand fall back.

"Nathan, I need your help."

Nathan's head popped up, and Henry could see his glassy eyes filled with unshed tears.

"Dad, why are you here? Why now?"

Answers flew through his head. He could tell Nathan he almost died and that he wanted to change. He wanted to tell him that he was here to make sure he didn't grow up alone like he did.

Instead, he went with the simple truth. "I love you, Nathan. I haven't always been the best father, and I know that, but I want to be there for you now."

Tears fell down his face. "For how long?"

Henry saw the tears and felt more helpless than he had in the hospital when he was waiting to find out if he had terminal cancer or not. "I'll stay as long as you want me to stay. I just want to get to know you and be in your life."

"And if I tell you to go?"

"Nathan—"

"If I said I didn't want you to stay here and to go away, would you?"

Henry swallowed and looked into the face of his only son. "Nathan, give me a chance. I'm not asking you to forgive me. I just want a chance for us to be—"

Nathan shook his head. "You're going to ruin it and leave me again. You say you want to do what I want, but if I ask you to go, you won't." Nathan jumped up and backed away. "Nothing is different. You'll make mom cry, and then you'll leave. You'll leave her, and you'll leave me!"

Henry stood up and tried to call to Nathan, but Nathan had turned and run away.

Henry sat back down on the grass and looked at the spread. He didn't stop the tears from falling. He looked to the sky and waited for something. The tension in his chest was building from the pain he had no way to express. He just sat there in the clearing, alone, and let the tears fall down his cheeks.

Fifteen

"Chocolate dipped strawberries are a go-to if you want to impress a woman and let her know it's serious," Adam said as he opened the tray of strawberries.

Hannah looked at the plump strawberries with intent. "We're supposed to be furthering the image of us being an item."

"We are. I guarantee you, as soon as I ordered these strawberries, there was a head count on who was missing and who would be receiving them. I'm telling you; this is the epitome of romance. Ask any guy."

Adam had shown up for the next date. It was a new feeling, knowing someone was planning events just for you. She was nervous and excited all at the same time. She'd dated of course, but it was accidental, and there were so many questions on whether or not she liked them.

With Adam, it was dating with intent. Knowing it was happening, she waited for his call or email that said to meet him. How could those silly little words make her feel so special? When she was alone and reflected on it, she called herself crazy. She called herself a fool to fall back into this trap. She knew her luck. She knew this was temporary. But every time she thought of Adam, she felt young, shy, and got the tingles that came with a new love.

Love and Adam should never be used in the same sentence. She had to remember he was helping her out.

They were sitting on a small hill outside. Normally she was comfortable outside, but this wasn't one of those moments. The hill sported a view of some farms and a clear view of the horizon. They had some finger foods, and she was second guessing if she should have packed a basket for them.

When he held a strawberry to her mouth, she hesitated. Then she took a bite and leaned back.

"Now explain to me how this is helping us."

"I can see you weren't born here in Sweet Blooms. If you were, you would know you're sitting where all the guys take girls when they want to sneak a kiss, and no one knows."

Hannah's mouth opened, and she stared at him. "You mean you brought me to a make-out spot?"

Adam laughed. "No one says that anymore, except for our generation, but as to the question, yes. I bought some strawberries, and we are at *the spot*, and yes, it is very clear to anyone looking that we are a serious item."

She looked around the place and then back at him. "Well, thank you. I think. I didn't know you were so good at planning." She gave him a clap. "Let me pay you for the strawberries. They must have cost a bit. They're huge and fresh."

"You like them?"

"Yes, so if you—"

"No, it doesn't work like that. We're dating, and I'm paying."

"But this is—"

"It's just what I said. The date I'm taking you on."

"If you're sure."

"I am. Now make sure you eat all of these strawberries."

"Worried they'll be wasted?"

Adam laughed. "No, this is how it works. I buy an impressive gift, and you eat it as a show of appreciation."

Hannah looked at the tray of six. "Well, it's good you got half because I only appreciate four and you'll have to help out."

Adam smiled. "I like a woman who isn't afraid to give some orders."

"O-kay." She reached in and grabbed a strawberry and held it to his mouth. "Eat up, buttercup!"

They settled into a moment of silence. He had his arm around her as he was finishing up the last strawberry. Then he leaned down and whispered, "We must be ever vigilant against those busybodies who know the secret techniques of spying."

"What are you talking about?" She turned to face him, and then he kissed her. One moment she was about to argue with him and this ridiculous notion that small towns were always watching, and then she was lost in his arms and in his kiss. She hadn't had time to prepare. Now she was just awash in feeling. It never ceased to surprise her. It started out as a small, warm spot that just spread in all directions. It left no part of her untouched, and without her realizing it, she found herself leaning into him more. Trying to find a way to get more of that feeling.

His arms tightened, but instead of feeling trapped, it deepened the moment and let her concentrate on how his lips moved over hers and how his lips teased her but didn't demand. She was safe and in control all at the same time.

He was stoking a fire of need that she hadn't felt in a while. She had wondered if she would ever feel it again, and here it was. She didn't second-guess—instead, she gave in to it and wrapped her arms around his waist.

Her hands traced his back, going over the muscles that moved ever so slightly under her hands. He was a force of nature, a place of refuge, and she wanted more.

More? What was she doing?

She had Nathan. She was a mother. Was she really about to make out at a make-out point?

Adam pulled back slowly, "I don't know, Hannah, you say I'm perfect, but I can tell I've just lost the girl," he said with a smile.

"What?"

"It's when your hands went from moving over me to your body stopping as if in a freeze-frame."

Embarrassed, she pulled back. "I'm sorry. I was thinking."

"Wow, I'm really losing my glow if kissing me makes you think about other things."

"Adam, stop. You don't need any more encouragement. I'd be surprised if there was anything anyone said you didn't do perfectly."

"Okay, if it's not me, what happened?"

Hannah heard him, and the concern was genuine. How could she explain to him that it was her? She was in danger of really caring for him. She was the problem here, not him.

He tipped her chin up to him and looked her in the eye. "We tell each other the truth, right? We're partners in crime it's you and me against the busybodies of Sweet Blooms. I've got your back, but you've got to tell me what it is that I'm fighting."

"Adam," she said in a small voice. "You're fighting me."

He brushed his thumb over her cheek. "Tell me."

"I'm a mother, and I'm here. I want the best for Nathan. I don't always make the best decisions, but I always think about what will be best for him. Here I am, and we're going off-script from our deal."

"Yes, you and the deal."

"It's about the deal, right? We still have a deal on what we're doing?"

Adam brushed her cheek one more time. "Yes, we'll do this your way." Heaving a big sigh, he kissed her on the forehead and then turned to pick up the empty container of strawberries.

"What are you doing?"

"I'm packing up."

She stared at him in shock, confused and worried she had done something wrong. When he faced her, he stopped and smiled.

"Stop thinking so hard. You're right; I wasn't thinking about Nathan. He's important, and I have to make sure I take him into consideration. You are an amazing mother, Hannah. I wouldn't have you any other way. I want you to know you're also an amazing woman. Let's go."

Hannah was warmed and frustrated at the same time. "We go when he says go. We leave when he says leave. I'm just waiting for you to grunt, and that will make your caveman persona complete."

Adam laughed. "You're so good for me, Hannah. You make me laugh. You're feisty too."

"Feisty? Who says feisty anymore?"

When they were both standing, he pulled her into his embrace and hugged her.

"Thank you, Hannah. I started this date for one reason, but I realize it's been a while since a woman went out on a date with Adam Cade and not the owner of Cade Designs."

She laid her head on his cheek and took a deep breath. "You're not so bad, Adam Cade, despite you having a lot of money."

They both laughed and packed up. Hannah knew something had changed today. She couldn't pinpoint exactly what it was, but she didn't want to dissect it and question it. She felt a little less alone in the world. The feeling was priceless.

Sixteen

"Hannah, your classes are booked again. There are some requests for private lessons and more classes. I'm sure if you also advertised you have a successful online business, it would boost enrollment for more classes," Sandra said. She looked at Hannah across the desk with that predatory smile. Sandra Waters was a nice woman. She was just a bit too aggressive for Hannah's taste when it came to getting business for the community center.

"Have you thought about letting them know about your online business?" Sandra asked again. Hannah rolled her eyes and thought, *You'd think if a person ignored a question, that would be the universal sign that it's not up for discussion.*

"I'm not ready to do that. I don't have any more time to give to classes and keep my business running," Hannah replied.

"Well, expansion, expansion, expansion; that's the way to go these days. You know the center is available for rental space if you need it to store your products, or if you need to get some people trained to assist you. Because you've been here for a while, I could definitely give you a discount."

Hannah smiled and nodded her head. "As soon as I think I'm ready, I'll make sure to let you know."

Hannah thought, *like never!*

"Have you spoken to Mr. Cade about his classes?"

It took everything Hannah had in her to not to say, "Back off, he just got here." Instead, she held her tongue and came out with a polite answer.

"Mr. Cade is still doing some planning. I think he mentioned this would be his long-term home and he didn't want to start anything that he couldn't maintain. He's very mindful of his potential students."

Sandra grinned. "Yes, I was very mindful of his potential too. His deep pockets suggest he could be a patron, or that he could open some sort of fund for us."

Hannah didn't say anything. She hoped that the comment would go by the wayside.

"Sandra, I've sat in one of his classes, and he's very careful and gives out instructions that are very clear, and he's patient."

Sandra looked at a paper on her desk. "He's going to have to be patient because I have a waitlist building for his woodworking class. It reads like the who's who of most eligible females in the neighborhood."

Hannah stared at her. "Are you serious?"

Sandra nodded. "I think we should create the classes sooner rather than later. So, talk to him about it, will you, Hannah?"

"Why the rush?"

"You know how people are with money. Today he's saying he'll be staying, but in a week or a month, who knows. He may decide the small country foray is over. The rich are hard to understand."

Hannah couldn't believe what she was hearing. "You

think because he has money, he can't be counted on to do the classes?"

"Listen, it's not that he won't try. The rich just get bored. So, you have to strike while the iron is hot."

Hannah knew her voice was getting tense, but she couldn't just let Sandra talk about Adam this way. What did Sandra know about Adam? Nothing! "I think you should give Adam some more credit. He made a lot of money by following through. Besides, it's not like he's a billionaire, and he's from Sweet Blooms."

Sandra stopped, closed the file on her desk, and gave Hannah a level gaze.

"We both know what Adam Cade is," she said.

"No, I don't think we do. Adam has gone to the council to apply like everyone else. He hasn't bought out a street or put his face on anything. He even interviewed with me for the class. He has good material. He knows his subject, and he doesn't mind working with kids. I don't know why you think he's so different."

"Adam Cade is part of the idle rich. Oh, he's back visiting his small town, but when he's passed this midlife crisis that he's having, he'll go back to the city. They will embrace him and keep him happy. Who leaves the city to come to Sweet Blooms? To be honest, Hannah, I don't know why you're making such a big deal about this."

"Sandra, I know what it's like for people to make assumptions about you just because you come from the city. I make sure everyone has to perform the same way to get a class in the center. I didn't give Adam any slack when he interviewed. If I had realized he wouldn't be given a fair chance and we would try to burn him out, I wouldn't have interviewed or offered him the spot here."

Sandra sniffed. "Listen, his classes are full, and the waiting list is growing. I'll start him with one class, but when he misses a class, I'll cancel the rest. He gets a chance."

"I don't think so," Hannah said. "From what you're saying, if he gets sick, he's out. If he has a family emergency, he's out. We have the same policy for all teachers. No excessive absence unless you have a good reason. He should have the same rules."

Sandra wasn't happy, but she agreed. "This will come back to haunt you, Hannah. You'll see that the rich just aren't like us."

"You don't even know; it was one of the few times I thought about taking her out to the back," Hannah said while talking to Skye. "You should have heard her. I was wondering when she would say 'stop calling him Mr. Cade and say Daddy Warbucks!' It was horrible, and she didn't seem to have any shame at all talking about him like that."

"Adam, is it?" Skye asked as she took a sip of her shake.

"Yes, that's his first name."

"Well, I hear you must know his name really well because I was in the general store and someone mentioned to Clarissa that there were some chocolate covered strawberries bought for a very special lady."

Hannah looked at the inquiring gaze from Skye and burst out laughing. Skye immediately sat up.

"Okay, I'll bite. What was so funny?"

Hannah covered her mouth and took a deep breath.

"He said people would notice the berries and I told him he was crazy."

Skye smiled. "Trust the man, he may know a thing or two. Now, back to you being outraged on his behalf and wanting to become the valkyrie incarnate to protect his honor and save his name."

Lunch was brought by the waitress in time to stop the staunch defense Hannah was about to launch. When the waitress left, Skye began.

"I've seen him, and it's hard not to notice he's attractive. I've also seen him in the papers going to the parties we hear about on television. So, I'm not saying Sandra is right, but I am saying I can see how she might not identify with him."

Hannah took a bite of her salad. "She said that he was here because he was going through some midlife rich-man crisis."

"Did that bother you because you were rooting for the underdog, or because you're starting to have feelings for him?"

Hannah stopped and looked at her best friend. "He's a good man, even though he did come from the city."

"Living in the city doesn't mean you have bad stock."

"What do you think?" Hannah asked.

"I think that life is short. When my brother passed away a year ago in the military, I realized there was so much that neither one of us had done. When I see that people have a chance to love and explore, I think they should take it."

Hannah looked at her with a raised eyebrow. "It's funny that you haven't left Sweet Blooms with that thought."

Skye smiled. "When Steven went to the Army, we wrote all the time. No matter where he was, we sent each other postcards and updates. I have postcards from all over the world. I lived through him for so long, and without him, I feel like I'm missing my other half. Life is made up of compromises. I'm trying to find the sweet ones to take advantage of."

For the rest of lunch, they talked about all of the gossips in town and the coming Summer Festival. It was a big event that the council went to. It was called the grown-up prom. Everyone waited to be invited by someone. Hannah was never invited, and she didn't wait for it anymore.

She had to think about what Skye said. She was making a list and guarding her heart the best way she knew how. Adam was here to help her, and then he would go on and find someone else. Hannah didn't want to look too closely at why the idea of him being with someone else sparked a deep grief she wasn't willing to name.

Henry had to do something. After the lunch with Nathan, the only thing he could think to do was to go to Hannah. He had to do something, or he had to leave, and leaving wasn't an option. He had been leaving every time something went wrong, and that hadn't been working all that well for him, so he was going to stay and fight. He'd camp on her doorstep if he had to. He kept ringing the bell. He'd already looked under the pot on the side of the door. The key was gone. He guessed everything had changed since he had lived here.

"I'm coming! Give me a moment," Hannah said as she opened the door.

"I wasn't sure if you were in the back or had just decided not to talk to me."

Henry saw Hannah roll her eyes. The problem was she didn't say it wasn't true. In fact, she hadn't said anything. With the door open, he took it as the okay to enter.

"Oh, where's your friend?" she asked.

"He's at the hotel. We don't travel everywhere. We had just arrived in town when you saw us."

Hannah led him to the living room. The meeting was already starting out uncomfortably. The living room was okay for guests, but people you knew, and family, were always brought to the kitchen.

"The house looks good," he said, taking a seat on the couch. "It's not the furniture that we had, but it's still good."

Hannah had on her gardening clothes. She wore a baggy shirt and worn jeans. Her hair was in a ponytail. He could see the random streaks of dirt on her face and neck.

Hannah nodded and shrugged. "Did you come to reminisce or tell me what's different with the house?"

"No. I came because of Nathan." Henry wanted to ask why she was so defensive. Hannah knew him, and he didn't understand why she didn't want to help him.

Hannah sat on the chair across from the couch. Her mannerisms reminded him of Nathan. He was reliving the afternoon with Nathan, and he was feeling defensive and attacked.

"Talk, Henry. You came about Nathan? I'm willing to listen."

"How can it be we are at this point? I'm not a bad person, Hannah."

She shifted in the chair and gave him a long look. "Do you really want to do this? I thought you came here for Nathan."

"I am here for Nathan, but I think it's impossible to separate the two. What are you telling him that he thinks I'm a bad person?"

Hannah rubbed her forehead and then sat back in the chair. "Okay, let's do this."

"Do what?"

Hannah smiled. "You know, when we were together, I thought you were the most amazing person ever. I thought you had great potential to do whatever you wanted to do. You know what, Henry? I have the same thought. You were always more outgoing and adventurous."

Hearing her say the words took the wind out of him. "I didn't hear it enough, Hannah. I felt like every time I did anything good it was because I was from a small town. The good in my life had nothing to do with the man."

"Henry, it was no secret that I wanted to leave the city. When we met, you told me story after story about us moving here. What did you want?"

Looking around the house, Henry saw memories of his father, and of lonely times in the house when no one cared if he was alive or dead. This town might be a great place for Hannah, but for him, it was full of memories of a father that was abusive and a mother who had left, not willing to deal with his father.

"Well, now you live here, and you own the house."

"I've started to rent out the rooms for the extra cash. It works for Nathan and me."

"So, I heard. Everyone has heard you are seeing Adam Cade. Do you think that's really wise?"

Hannah drew in a breath. "I'm not going there. Why did you come to Sweet Blooms?"

"I had a cancer scare. I was in the hospital, and no one came to see me."

"You had a scare? So, you're fine?"

He looked at her still sitting in her chair. No exclamations, no 'oh my goodness,' nothing. "Yes, I'm fine. Like I said, it was just a scare. I had some exploratory work, and they removed some benign tumors that had been building up.

"During that time, I realized that no one had come to see me. No one knew where I was or what I was doing. You know I've been making some money in real estate and selling the last couple of years. I mean, I have to keep a lot in liquid to make the best deals, but it's been working for me. I think I finally found something that I'm good at."

Hannah smiled. "I'm happy for you, Henry. I know you were searching for a long time for something you could call your own."

Henry cleared his throat. Then he clapped his hands and opened them. "All of that is behind me. What matters now is, after that incident, I realized what was important. Nathan is important to me."

"Henry, children aren't switches that you can turn on and then turn off. It doesn't work that way. It takes time and trust for children to understand you'll be there, and they can count on you."

"He trusts you. Tell him to trust me, to give me a boost. If we work together, you can help me with Nathan. We can go do things fathers and sons do. I'm sure when we're together more, he'll like football. I mean, when he can throw a ball, he'll really like football."

Hannah shook her head. "It doesn't work like that."

"What do you mean? He's a child. I remember being one of those, you know. You tell him what to do, and he does it."

Hannah's expression was one of displeasure. "What could I say now? I don't bully Nathan into doing things. I discuss them with him, and we decide on what we're going to do."

"Really? Did you decide you were going to give my son to another man? I see you're deciding to see Adam Cade. What is it? Are you finally tired of this little town? I know he's got a lot of money."

Hannah stood up. "We're done."

"I think the rustic look working in the garden is a bit much, but if that's the way you want to go..."

Hannah plastered a smile on her face and opened the front door. "Thank you for stopping by. I'll let Nathan know you were here. If you want to see him, you have his number, so give him a call. I will make myself scarce so you two can get to know each other."

Henry held out his hands in the doorway. "Maybe I assumed too much. I'm just trying to connect with my son."

Hannah shooed him across the threshold of the door until he was on the outside. "I have no problem with you wanting to see Nathan again. How you build that relationship is up to you. I would never try to replace you with another man. If you thought it was possible, then you don't really know me at all.

"The thing I think you need to remember the most is this: Nathan isn't just your son. That means he may not like football, whether he can throw or not. He may not like football ever. In fact, it might do you some good to read some recipes. Nathan likes to cook. Nathan isn't yours, and he's not mine. Nathan is *our* son. A gift. And you'd better remember that before you lose it."

With those words, she slammed the door in his face. He looked at the door and leaned his head against it. He had blown it. His mouth had run away from him, and here he was. Outside and alone.

Seveteen

"You had to hear him," Hannah railed before cutting her steak as if she were trying to disembowel it. "He thinks he can just appear, and it will all be better."

Adam watched her tear into the meal he had prepared. Nathan had received an invitation from one of her friends from school. Hannah was thrilled, and when she had invited him over, he thought she wanted to have a date with him. He shouldn't have had hoped that high.

"You mean when he showed up earlier this week or last night?" he asked.

"Both! He has always been the same. He accused me of wanting the small town instead of him. He criticized the furniture. How could he? Maybe he didn't remember that I sold the furniture on his say-so because he had said he didn't want the old memories. He wanted to know if my clothes were a ruse to get you. It's so apparent that he knows what kind of woman you would be attracted to."

"He doesn't know a thing if he thinks I'd change anything about you."

Hannah stopped waving her fork around in indignation. "You're pretty good with those lines, you know. Is that a corporate thing, thinking fast on your feet?"

"Thank you, but I have to tell you it's an, I have a sister thing, and I've got to use what I've got."

Hannah smiled. "Maybe, but CeeCee seems really nice."

Shaking her head, Hannah took another bite of her steak and swallowed.

"I know I complain about him, but I do feel bad that he was alone when he thought he was sick." She had told him about the scare while they were setting the table. "You'd think he would be a little more grateful that the outcome wasn't a bunch of malignant tumors."

Adam put some green beans on her plate. "I think the both of you are in a bad spot. You feel bad he was in the hospital alone, but you're still concerned he hasn't changed enough to be around Nathan. He wants to have a relationship with his son but thinks the only gateway would be through you. It's not easy on any side."

Hannah stopped and looked Adam in the eye. "I don't know that I could be that objective. I mean, I agree with you, but seeing it from both sides, I just haven't grown up that much. Things are better now, but I remember what it was like trying to explain to Nathan that his father wasn't showing up even though we had been waiting all day. And then he'd finally remember to call and cancel. That was for the days he did remember to cancel.

"I want him to go and leave us alone. Now that it's better, he'll just ruin it."

Adam reached out to tuck a strand of hair behind her ear. "Can he really do that?"

Hannah groaned. "No, he can't. I just want peace of mind then." She sighed. "Enough. He's ruining a great dinner. Why don't we talk about you?"

"Me?"

"I realized when I took your sister to the airport that we haven't talked about the secret plans you're building out on your land."

"It's no secret. I want to build my apprentice shop on my property. I have space, and it will let me work late in the shop if I want and be close to home."

"I hear a 'but' in there."

"No buts. I just need to assign the project manager. I chose one. His name is Pierce. He's from a company that I've used before."

"If you've used them before, why don't you sound relieved with the decision?"

"I felt like I should have hired a local, but logic said to go with someone who has done this sort of work before."

"I would trust your feelings. Your feelings brought you out here. Shouldn't you follow them to get the work done as well?"

Adam shrugged. "It's done. I'll see it as it goes forward."

"Okay, so you have a project manager. What, exactly, is he managing? Are you building your company all over again?"

Adam laughed. "No, that is exactly what I don't want. I'm looking to offer some apprenticeships for kids who don't do as well in school. I wasn't a scholar, but I found a niche working with my hands."

"I've looked at the sign-ups for your class. You have a waiting list."

Adam shrugged. "The list doesn't scare me."

"Really? Have you seen the list?"

"It's all the same. They aren't even coming to the class for the first two weeks. I think my drop-out rate will be high when all the women who signed up realize there will be a test and work required."

"You've looked at the list?"

Adam nodded. "If the rumors are true, it's every single female under thirty who lives in Sweet Blooms."

Hannah looked down at her plate. "Well, that would help you find someone. You won't have to go anywhere; they will come to you."

He reached across the table and looked her in the eye. "You are more than enough. While we are doing this, there will be no one else for me." Hannah leaned into his hand.

"This isn't a normal thing, so I understand," she whispered in a low voice.

"I heard you, Hannah, and my answer is still the same. I'm with you and only you until you tell me otherwise."

Hannah thought about what Adam had said the night before. When Nathan came into the kitchen for breakfast, she knew she had to address the issue they hadn't really talked about.

"Nathan, I think we need to talk."

"Yeah, mom?"

"I saw your father yesterday."

Nathan started to stand and leave the table. "Can we talk about it later? I have to meet up with—"

"Nathan, this isn't going away."

Nathan looked at his mother and then took a seat. "I tried. I saw him, and he doesn't know me. Why does this matter? You don't like him, so why should I?"

Hannah took a seat at the table and then put her hands over his.

"Nathan, I think it's important that you have a relationship with your father."

"You don't like him!"

Hannah looked into her son's face and saw the frustration and confusion in his eyes. She had to wonder when this had happened. It had always been the two of them, but she hadn't meant to poison a son against his father.

"Nathan, your father and I don't get along for a lot of reasons. That doesn't mean you can't like him. It doesn't mean that the two of you won't get along."

"He left us. You always say we need to stick together. Even at school, you said if the people who say they are my friend leave at the slightest problem, they aren't the kind of people I want to have around me. Why is he different? He's just messing things up again!"

Nathan tried to tug his hands away from her. Instead, she stood up and pulled her son into her embrace. She felt his body rack with frustrated tears.

"Nathan, sometimes I complain out loud, but that doesn't mean your dad doesn't want you. I can tell you when you were born, he cried."

Nathan pushed away from her. "He cried?"

"Yes, he cried. He was so happy to see you. He didn't have the best relationship with his father, and he wanted to do right by you."

Nathan wiped his face. "Then why did he leave me?"

Hannah let out a sigh. "Do you remember when you had your goldfish?"

Nathan looked a bit confused. "Yeah, I remember."

"You remember you wanted to make sure it had fresh water, so you left it outside."

Nathan shook his head and flushed with embarrassment. "I do remember that, and the neighborhood cat ate him."

"You didn't mean for the goldfish to get hurt, but it did. I think parents are the same way. We do things for our kids that we think will work. Sometimes we ask for advice, and sometimes we think we just know. In the end, it doesn't work out as well as we thought."

"Are you going to see him again? I thought you were seeing Adam Cade?"

"Sit down; we might as well get this out of the way. What have you heard about Adam Cade?"

Nathan smiled. "You know I don't gossip. My mother taught me better, but if I was one of those people, I'd tell you Adam Cade has got way more money than we could spend in a lifetime. Some girls say he looks okay, but that's it."

Hannah smirked at him. "I'm glad you don't gossip. Adam and I are friends."

Nathan's smile got wider. "Okay, mom."

"Nathan be serious! You know I thought you'd be—"

"Be what?"

"I was nervous to say anything," she confessed.

Nathan smirked. "I'm almost thirteen."

"And?"

"I'm just saying, now that I'm a teenager, almost, I understand these things."

"Whatever," she said with a smile.

"When I couldn't play ball, you were okay. When I wanted to cook, you were okay. I know you don't think so, but I do have friends. I don't see any of yours. I think it's nice that you have a friend. And if the people your age call it 'being friends,' that's okay with me."

Hannah ruffled his hair. "Off with you! I have work to do and remember to give your dad a chance. I'm going to do the same. Love you, Nathan."

"Love you too, mom."

<h1 style="text-align:center">Eighteen</h1>

It was late in the afternoon, and Hannah was done teaching. Adam had come by after meeting with Pierce over the contracts and changes that needed to be done. They both agreed they were having a hard day and for once they wanted to be alone. Adam had brought a long sandwich and a large salad for them to share.

Adam still had dust on his jeans and was wearing a black tee shirt. It didn't detract a thing from him, according to Hannah.

"Thanks," she said as she took the first bite.

"For?"

"For coming out here. It's been a day. Today was my beginner class. You would be totally amazed at how many ways a person can make a knot. How's your day going?"

"My sister is settling in, and the board members are trying to find a way to manage her. I should have mercy on them and tell them it can't be done."

"Are you okay with your sister taking over? No last-minute thoughts on if you should go back?"

He reached out and tugged on her ponytail. "I have lots of thoughts, but none of them are regrets about coming to Sweet Blooms."

Hannah smiled. "I'm glad—"

Her words were interrupted by the one person she wasn't ready to face.

"Hannah?" Henry said from the doorway.

Hannah couldn't believe her bad luck. She had done the right thing with Nathan the night before. Oh, it hadn't felt good, and she was still smarting from holding her tongue, but if she was honest with herself—and she tried to be all the time—the problems between her and Henry should stay between her and Henry.

She turned around to find Henry standing there. "Hello, Henry."

Adam tipped his head toward him. "We didn't meet formally, I'm Adam Cade."

Henry gave him a long look and nodded. "There wasn't a need to introduce yourself. When the small-town guy done well comes home, everyone knows him. Hannah, I thought we could talk."

Hannah took a deep breath. "I think we should talk too, but not now."

"When do you want to talk then?" Henry turned towards Adam. "I'm sorry to interrupt, but Hannah and I have a son, and she finds it very hard to find time to speak to me."

"Really, Henry?" Hannah asked incredulously.

Adam put a hand on Hannah's shoulder. "What do you want, Henry?" Adam asked with a firm, clear voice. It stopped Hannah from moving and made Henry take notice of Adam.

"I just want my son in my life."

Adam nodded. "I think it's a good thing to strive for. Hannah can't be that bridge for you."

Henry looked confused and looked from Adam to Hannah. "Hannah has always done that. She's always been the one who could talk to Nathan."

"You need to do that on your own."

Hannah was spellbound by Adam's words. She was equally caught by the idea that Henry was listening to Adam.

"Who are you? If I can talk to Hannah, we'll fix this."

"I'm Adam."

"I told you I know your name. Who are you to Hannah?"

Hannah held her breath. This was the time that Adam could say he was a friend. He could say he was helping her out. She stiffened her spine and waited. She would survive whatever he said and deal with Henry.

"I'm the man in her life, for as long as she'll have me," Adam said.

Henry backed up. "You're serious about Hannah?"

"We are definitely an item."

Adam spoke so clearly that Hannah was convinced it was true. Well, it wasn't like it wasn't true, but it wasn't the complete truth and, well, it didn't matter. What mattered was the warm and soft fuzzies that were going through her body.

Henry looked between them, and his anger turned to laughter. Hannah turned to face him but backed away. It was this moment that she had been trying to outrun. The moment when everyone could see she was different or didn't fit in and they laughed. She didn't want this moment to ever come for Nathan, and now that it was here for her, it hurt just as much as she thought.

When Adam spoke, he had steel in his voice. "What's funny?"

"I can understand Hannah wanting to be with you, but you wanting Hannah?"

Hannah just closed her eyes. Deep inside, she knew Henry was lashing out because she was with Adam. It didn't make it hurt any less. It didn't make the embarrassment any less. She just waited for the ground to open up or for Henry to go away.

"Ah, now it's clear why you two aren't together. Hannah is the most amazing contradiction of a woman that a man could ever hope to have. She's smart and independent, but she lets me take care of her. She knows what she wants but has the patience to let me set the pace. She's beautiful, and an amazing mother. She listens when I would fight, and she fights for those who don't deserve it.

"I want to thank you for being irresponsible and selfish and only thinking of you. Without you blowing it, I would have missed the woman of a lifetime."

Hannah looked at Adam and knew she'd be able to say it all changed at that moment. She understood Adam was a good man, and he was doing what he thought was the right thing, but Hannah would never look at him the same.

Henry cleared his throat. "Well, I'm obviously the intruder here. I'll see my way out."

Hannah waited until he was gone before she spoke.

"Thank you for sticking up for me," she said quietly.

"You make it sound like there was another option," he said as he picked up a part of the sandwich.

Hannah nodded. "Of course, there wasn't an option. You're not that type of guy."

"Hannah, I have to tell you something."

"Yes?" she whispered.

"Look at me, please," Adam asked.

Hannah took a deep breath and looked at him.

"You're an amazing woman. I didn't say what I said because it was the right thing. I didn't do it because of that deal in your head either. I said it because it's the truth. I said it because you are stronger than you know, and you're beautiful on the inside and out."

"Adam, thank you nonetheless."

"I wish the world didn't have men who are slow to recognize a treasure when they have one, but we do. You've been around a person who didn't see the treasure you are. Henry is lost and alone. He's trying to play catch up, and the game's almost over."

She looked at Adam eating away. "Don't make me feel bad for him."

Adam shrugged. "I'm just telling you what I see. No matter what happens, you and Henry will always have a bond in Nathan. You may not like a lot of things, but you will have to find a way to deal with him."

"I guess you mean waiting him out until he leaves isn't an option?"

Adam laughed. "No, it's not, because you are stronger than that. You don't run from trouble."

Hannah immediately got her hackles up. "I don't run, I'm just voicing my opinion very loudly."

"What did I do to Luke to make him put me here?"

Katherine looked around the space and then went back out the front door of a building on Adam's land. It was the first time he'd ever seen Luke's wife Katherine, rattled. He would have to tell Luke he was right.

If he wanted to get Katherine out of her shell, this move certainly had done that.

Katherine looked at him with a raised eye. "Did you help Luke do this?"

He held his hands up and backed away. "No, I didn't plan this. I asked him why was he relocating you, and he assured me it was the right thing and something you needed."

Katherine ran her hand through her hair. "Am I to understand that this building we are constructing is the best place to open up the base site? He's an accountant, and he can count, but he won't count on me showing up at his door unexpectedly."

Adam grinned, trying not to laugh out loud. Luke and Katherine would be in this location. This building would hold the accounting office and the apprentice rooms as well.

"We are going to put in some comforts, so it will be better. This is the preliminary look."

Katherine turned on him, and even Adam had to take a step back. "So, it won't be so bad. I'll be stuck in a building where they cut wood all day long. So, the cutting machines will go all day and most of the night for the people who are dedicated. When the whirring noise isn't going on, then the fine dust of wood will float in the air, so when you open the door to talk to us, that film of wood dust will get on everything."

"I'm open to new ideas."

"How about we keep the office in New York?"

Adam smiled and shook his head. "New York? You've been there and done that. You don't want to do the same old thing over and over again."

"I think I like the repetition. Besides, have you been

in town? It's like a horror show. They're all happy. The children are running around with no parents. The little kids run around with no leashes on them. The single people are actually located in one place because they 'need help'. I think the town goal is for them all to marry and make more happy people. Do you know they have a coffee house that doesn't have the stock market playing in it?"

Adam stopped and caught Katherine's gaze. "Katherine, I need you. I have to focus on the practical side, and I need to know the business isn't slipping away. I'll make a deal with you. If you stay for a year and you still don't like it, I'll work something out. But right now, there isn't anyone else besides Luke that I would trust to help me set this up. Will you stay?"

Katherine moaned. "Why do you have to be a nice guy? If you had laid down the law, I would have been able to topple you over. Okay, I'll stay, but I just want us all to know that this was under duress and it's temporary."

Adam hugged Katherine. "Thanks. While you're here, I need you to watch someone. I hired a project manager, and I need your insight."

Adam and Katherine kept talking for another hour. When it was done, Adam felt better that he had another set of eyes to help him get this right.

Nineteen

Adam's words settled over her. She knew that Adam was right. For Nathan's sake, if for no other reason, she had to find a way to make peace with Henry. Nathan had made dinner and went to his aunt Pamela's for the night. She had sat down with Nathan and asked him if he would cook, and he had taken time to carefully select the meal. Tonight's dinner was fried chicken, mashed potatoes, green beans, and for dessert, apple pie.

She looked at the table and, for a moment, thought about canceling. She could just not open the door. Maybe try again later. She shook her head and threw off the notion of running. This wasn't for her. It was for Nathan.

When the bell rang, she took a breath and went to make amends with her past. Why did this walk feel like the death row walk?

"Henry," she said as she stepped aside for him to enter.

"Hannah."

Henry was true to form. He came in a plaid shirt and blue jeans. He had a bouquet of flowers that he shoved into her hands.

"I got these for you. I remembered you like flowers."

Hannah had to bite back a response. She couldn't stand flowers. To her, it was the gift of dying flowers. She pasted a smile on her face and thanked him. Hannah found a vase and put the flowers in it. She had to stay upbeat for this to work.

Henry followed her into the house and watched her put the flowers up. "The food smells good."

Hannah smiled and looked at him. "It was made by Nathan."

She could see the surprise on his face. "Nathan made a whole meal?"

Hannah smiled. "He did. We joke that the reason he's such a good cook is because I'm such a bad one."

Henry followed Hannah into the kitchen. He saw the set up for two and smiled.

"I thought you were going to talk to me for five minutes, lay down the law, and kick me out."

Hannah heard him and laughed. "No, I'll feed you so you can experience how great a chef Nathan is and then think about tossing you out."

She set the table and laid out the food. They ate in silence for a minute before Henry spoke.

"The food is good. I didn't know he liked cooking that much."

"He does it as a hobby. When he does, I'm so grateful. Nathan is really talented at whatever he applies himself to."

Hannah wasn't good at waiting, and she wanted to make sure she didn't have to do this kind of thing again without Nathan.

"I'm surprised you came back. I know you had no love for the town, considering your past."

Henry nodded. "That's true. Situations change, and I

didn't want my past to stop me from getting to know my son."

"Henry, I want you to get to know Nathan too."

Henry put down his fork. "Have I really been that distant?"

"Let's just say your timetable is to drop a note every month. Young boys live day to day."

Henry nodded. "Why doesn't Nathan do more boy things?"

Hannah was about to jump out of her seat in defense of Nathan, but she took a breath and let the red clear. "I don't push Nathan to do one thing over the other. I help him when I can, but I'll tell you that he's a very giving person. He works with making food for the elderly, and he's on the track team here in Sweet Blooms."

Henry cleared his throat. "I think Nathan is fine, Hannah. It's hard for me to see him and think I could do this or that, but I can't. He's got his own personality, and I may not fit into his life now."

"Henry, when you get to know Nathan, you'll see he is the best of us both."

Henry laughed. "You see something in me that's good. I didn't expect that."

"Henry, when it comes to diving in and giving it all you've got, I have to tell you I admire your conviction and discipline. It comes at a cost. Everyone and everything has to take a second seat."

Henry picked over his mashed potatoes. "This guy, Adam Cade, isn't that way?"

Hannah stopped and looked at him. "Are we going there again?"

Henry held his hands up in surrender. "I was wrong when I spoke last time. I was angry with you."

"Henry, why? We're not together, and we've both moved on."

Henry blew out a breath. "I was angry because it looked like you had it all. I can't talk to my own son, Hannah. You live with Nathan, and you seem to have the rich guy in town. I can't compete with that. I don't want to be replaced by Adam in Nathan's life. I'm concerned about you too."

"Me?"

"Yeah, I know you were born in the city, but men with money are a different breed. They hang out with different kinds of women, and everyone knows the rules. You're not like that."

Hannah listened to Henry, and she heard Sandra's words all over again. "You're judging him, and you don't know him."

Henry reached across the table and covered her hand with his. "I'm not judging. I'm looking out for you. I've been around a bit, and you haven't. You don't understand. Adam was with Nadia, one of the most beautiful women in the world. He may be okay with you here for a little while, but do you think this place will keep him?

"He has women at his beck and call. Those women are models, business owners, they're movers and shakers on a world platform. Even when you two are out, you must notice the attention you attract.

"Think about the signs. He'll want to go to private places when you two are together. That's nothing more than him protecting his image. You're a nice person; it wouldn't occur to you. I know these men, and that's what they do. I'm saying this to make sure you and Nathan are okay. I don't want you to be another broken heart on his path."

Hannah didn't know how but she held in the howl of despair and doubt. She smiled and nodded at Henry. Later, she couldn't remember what had happened during the rest of meal to save her life. She just remembered nodding and telling Henry how great Nathan was. When Henry was at the door, he turned to Hannah.

"Thank you, Hannah. I don't know if I have anything to offer Nathan. I want you to know I've been listening, and before I decide if I want to make a push in his life, I'll let you know and make sure I can offer something. A lot depends on my work. Real estate isn't big business in Sweet Blooms."

Hannah nodded. "Think about it, Henry. If you keep Nathan as the main goal, I'm sure you'll come to the right decision."

After all the pleasantries had been exchanged, she closed the door. Hannah leaned her head against the door and slid down until she was on the floor. Henry's words came back and taunted her. She thought about how Adam had taken her to the private spots so the "busybody" couldn't find them.

She was a naïve fool. She had thought there was something between them, but all along she was a case to be hidden. She pulled herself up and went to her bedroom. When she got to her bed, she curled in a ball and let the tears flow over her cheeks. The pain was so intense that she just held on to her pillow and rocked.

How could she have humiliated herself so much by throwing herself on this man who would have never noticed her otherwise?

Hannah was finished for the day. She wasn't really as present as she wanted to be. The words from last night were still in her head.

"Thanks for covering the crochet class," Sandra said to Hannah.

"It's no problem. I can do the basic classes," Hannah replied.

"I don't know if I told you, but all the people you've referred here have been consistent and brought in a steady income to the center. Thanks."

Hannah nodded in acknowledgment.

"By the way, Hannah, I wanted to ask you if you wanted to go to the Spring Festival."

Hannah smiled and nodded. "I'd love to come to the Festival."

Sandra put her hand to her head. "I'm so silly, of course you'll be at the festival because you're on the council. But if you want to sit with us, find us and we'll save you a spot."

"Thanks." Hannah looked away so no one would see the tears that threatened to fall. This was what she had been working towards. How ironic it was that she had finally gotten what she was looking for. She didn't need to embarrass herself or put Adam in an uncomfortable position anymore by being with her.

"By the way, today was the first introduction class by Adam. I went to survey it. He did a great job of keeping everyone focused. He took control of the classroom and paired people up to help them do the curriculum." Sandra had a sad grin on her face. "You know, when I mess up, I do it big. You were right. Adam is here for the love of what he does. I need to give him a chance. I thought for sure his true colors would come out when he got into the classroom, and he'd be flirting with the women or doing something outlandish like that. I was wrong and letting him have his classes here will be a boost for him and us."

"Thank you."

There it was. Everything she wanted to accomplish was here. The invite was the town's seal of approval. Adam had helped her to see that Henry was a necessary pain, but one she needed to deal with for Nathan's sake. He had given her so much. Made her feel so special. She wouldn't inconvenience him by holding him to their agreement.

Hannah knew it was time. She knew when he stood up for her, she was going past their agreement. Their agreement said they'd show solidarity and held each other's hand. Hannah felt like he was tying his reputation to hers by defending her so succinctly. She'd done the one thing she said she wouldn't do. Somewhere along the way, Hannah had 'caught feelings' for Adam Cade. It wasn't his fault; he was just a good man who was trying to help out a woman in a bad spot.

She wasn't looking forward to it, but she knew it had to be done sooner rather than later. She stood outside the center and waited for him to come out.

"Adam, over here," she called. Today had been a beast of a day. It was the first class, and the women were worse than bill collectors in their tenacity. He would explain what to do, and they would deliberately say they needed some additional help. When it was clear no work would be done, he decided to take another approach. He started pairing up members in the class, and all of a sudden the comprehension grew in his class.

Seeing Hannah was a relief. He had tried to talk to her during lunch, but she had rushed off. If he didn't know any better, he would have thought she was trying to avoid him, but that didn't make any sense at all.

He saw Hannah look both ways until all the students had cleared out. Adam could see she was waiting, and this didn't sit well with him. He knew something was coming. He braced himself for it. Maybe it was Clarissa trying her games again? He didn't know, but whatever it was, they had been talking things out; they'd do the same thing now.

Hannah looked at him and blinked a couple of times. He wanted to reach out and make her feel better, but she took a step back. "I wanted you to know I got invited to the Festival. You know that's the sign that I'm good with the town," she said. "You've been really kind with helping me out and taking the time to be seen with me."

Adam smiled. "It's been a pleasure."

Hannah didn't return his smile. In fact, if it was possible, she seemed sadder. "Well, the thing is, we don't have to do this anymore. You know, you won't be tied to me and have to do the dating thing and all of that."

He didn't move, he just listened to what she said and took in her body language—the glassy eyes and the fidgeting hands. "When did you decide this?"

"I think when the decision was done doesn't really matter here. When I think back on this, I realize that I really shouldn't have asked you in the first place. It was a huge inconvenience for you, as you are trying to get your life together."

"If it was a problem, I would have told you. I'm a grown man."

Something was very wrong here. Spending time with Hannah had made him realize what he wanted in a woman. It made him see how good they could be together. More importantly, it helped him to understand that it was possible to have someone be with him and not his money. He thought this was going in the right direction. She was the only woman he had considered since Nadia. Now she was saying it was done.

"I want you to know I don't know another guy who would have done what you've done and been as committed to me as you have been."

"What did I miss?" he said in a low voice. "Who got to you, Hannah?"

She popped her head up and looked him in the eye. When they were looking at one another, he could see her licking her lips and blinking away tears. "This is about us."

"You forget, Hannah, that I worked in corporate and ran a multi-million-dollar company. It's one of my jobs to know when people are lying. You need more time in if you want to fool me."

"I'm not lying. I'm trying to do the right thing."

Adam took a breath and thought about it. This was Hannah. Who could do this to her? Who would she walk away for? He knew Nathan wanted what was best for her. He had had a brief conversation with him, and he thought he had started on good footing there. That only left one person: the lost ex.

"What did Henry say?"

Hannah opened her mouth and then shook her head. "This is about us. I'm done with our deal. Are we clear?"

"Crystal," he bit out. "We are crystal clear."

He couldn't talk to her now. She had managed to rip apart his hopes for the future. Hannah was spooked, and he couldn't bulldoze his way through this. He needed a plan. He needed a plan to fight for what they had. He hoped she was ready to fight for them too.

Twenty

Henry was done. He had gotten his duffel bag out and just needed to figure out where he was going to go. Caleb had left a few days ago. He said he had to pick up something. Henry wasn't surprised. Caleb was an odd duck anyway. Henry thought he would be here when Caleb came back, but what was the point? He didn't have a reason to be here anymore.

He had already tried to drown his sorrows, and it had gone poorly. It was times like this he wished he had a real vice. He had never taken to drinking because of his father. When he had tried to drown his woes, it was with a red glass of wine. He did it in the privacy of his room. He tried to think on all of the adversity he had overcome. He had entered into the real estate game late, but he had found a niche talking to people and settling them. He had faced the possibility of cancer and hadn't broken. All of that seemed small and inconsequential when compared to losing his son.

He had thought about what all of them had said. Maybe he could be a good father-like image in a big brother program. If anyone would have him, he could try to find a partner. When he thought on it, having a partner had helped Hannah out.

Maybe he'd join one of those traveling groups. He was bound to find some friends there. If he could make some friends, at least he wouldn't die alone.

He heard a sharp knock on the door. Henry went to it, rolling his eyes. He had told the front desk he was leaving. Maybe they wanted him out sooner. The way his luck had been running, Henry wouldn't be surprised.

When he opened up the door, he saw Caleb. He didn't bother hiding his shock. When Caleb took a step towards him, he stepped aside so Caleb could enter. He watched Caleb take in an assessment of the room and then turned to him.

"So, you're quitting?" Caleb said.

"I'm doing what's best," he answered. He wondered how long this would take. He didn't need this kind of thing from anyone, least of all Caleb. Besides, who was Caleb and why had he even come with him?

"I was hoping you weren't going to take the easy way out and run," he said.

Henry looked at the duffel and then thought about how much he didn't know. He didn't know his own son. He didn't know how this was going to end.

Caleb took a seat in his room, and Henry closed the door. "Did things get rough?"

Caleb's tone was starting to annoy him. "Things aren't rough, they're impossible. I've waited too long, and now it's just out of control. You don't understand! You can't understand."

"What I understand is commitment and dedication. You have to have that if you want something to work.

You really need that if you love something or someone," he said quietly.

"You think I don't know that? You think I came to this decision lightly? My son has a life, and I don't know it or him. He doesn't want me in his life. He's already asked me to leave," he said, as he sat on the edge of the hotel bed.

"Henry, let me tell you that I think you are a self-centered and self-serving person. You manage to do that without having a mean bone in your body. If you really care, you'll stay and find a way." With that, Caleb stood up and went to the door.

"Caleb, I have to ask, why the talk and why are you here?"

Caleb turned. "I promised a friend I would deliver something to someone in this town. He passed away, and he asked me to deliver it at a certain time. Promises are hard to keep. Even harder when the promise asks you to do something that is against your nature. But the measure of a man is how well he keeps his word. So, no matter how uncomfortable it makes me, I'll make sure to do this thing that was asked of me.

"If I would do this for a friend, I have to think how much more important it is that you do this for your son."

With that, Caleb walked out and left Henry in the room. Henry went to his bag and picked it up. His mind was made up.

If she had everything she wanted, why was she curled up on a Friday night nursing a broken heart? She couldn't remember a time she had felt this miserable.

She didn't want to bring Nathan's mood down too. He had begun to receive some invites from the guys at school, and they were trying to get him to make desserts for them to impress some girls. It wasn't smooth yet, but he was on his way.

So why did she feel so bad? Since she'd told him it was over, she hadn't seen Adam at all. The day after, she had come home to find a check and a note that said he was moving into his house. Of course, the move only fed into her belief that she had done the right thing. She knew she had made the right decision, but right now it felt awful. She was lonely. Her house and garden were filled with memories of him. When had he become a part of everything?

He had come in as a tenant. When his grandmother left, they had become partners. Now she was alone. How could all of this have happened on Henry's say so? Was she foolish to let Henry's words get to her? The problem with the words was that they made sense.

Did he miss her? Hannah didn't just miss her dating partner; she missed her friend. How funny to think this would be so much easier if he was ugly and broke. Attributes she would usually be so good at finding in a man.

She went downstairs to find some solace in her refrigerator. There was still some apple pie left. She could at least finish that up. She had just gotten the pie out on the table when she heard her bell. Hannah looked up. Was the world conspiring against her? She could ignore it and get her slice and go back upstairs. Yeah, she could—

"Hannah, it's me. Open up!" Adam called from the other side of the door.

She froze. Could she make it upstairs without him knowing? Why was he here? What if he forgot something and was here to pick it up?

She pulled herself together and went to open the door. As soon as she saw him, the gloom lifted, and the world became a better place. He looked more edible than the pie in the kitchen. She'd missed those solid tees across his chest and those dark jeans that always looked like he had just bought them. It was his look that wasn't in sync.

He had that look that said he wasn't angry, just frustrated. It was the look you had when the person in front of you emptied out all of their change in their purse because they didn't want to break the twenty-dollar bill to give the cashier twenty-seven cents.

"We're going to try this again, and I'm hoping that this time you can be a little more truthful," he said as he stepped into the house.

"Try what?"

"You know that Henry is wounded. You let something he said get in between us. I don't know what he said, but I'm here for us. The us that I want, and the us that I thought we were working on."

Hannah nibbled on her lower lip. "How did you know it was Henry?"

"That part wasn't rocket science. He's worried and jealous about his place with his son. He thinks controlling you is the answer. What was it? Did he say I was taking advantage of you?"

Hannah tried to cover her mouth from the laugh that came out. "You are so funny sometimes."

He reached out and tucked her hair behind her ear. "I thought we were in this together. You can't listen to them on the outside. They want what we have. I thought I was clear about how I felt about you. The day I defended you to Henry, it wasn't for show. I knew then you were the one."

"Why didn't you say it?"

"I thought I did!"

Hannah looked him in the eye. "I don't do hints. I need words. I don't do social cues either. I'm a plain-spoken person, and I need some plain speaking."

He leaned down and brushed his mouth over hers.

"You are the one I want to be with."

The second time he bent to kiss her, she was ready. When their lips met, she parted for him, and their tongues entwined. The warm wave of need spread through her body and her hands traced the outside of her arms until they met around his neck. He was strong and familiar to her.

He drew back.

"I don't want to pretend I don't need a shield. I need you, Hannah, with me. I need you as my friend, and I need you as my partner. Are you okay with that?"

Hannah stared back into his eyes, seeing the truth reflected in their depths.

"You know I come with Nathan."

"Great kid. He likes me. I know because he told me so," Adam bragged.

"Whatever," she joked. "You know I also come with Henry."

Adam closed his eyes and leaned his forehead against hers.

"Yes, I know, and you're so worth it."

"Well then, now that that has been settled, you should feed me."

"Huh?"

"All of this moaning over you and not knowing had me going on a fast. Now we should fix that and celebrate."

He grabbed her when she got ready to spin away. And he kissed her again.

"From now on, it's us two."

"Yes, this will be our own sweet beginning right here in Sweet Blooms."

Epilogue

He was sitting in the corner where no one would notice him. He was a consummate observer of life, and Sweet Blooms had that. There was a celebration going on. Hannah Jenkins and Adam Cade had announced their public secret—they were an item.

The lack of privacy was one of the many things Caleb didn't like about small towns. It didn't matter what he liked or didn't like; he was here to fulfill a promise. The object of that promise was working on the floor of the local restaurant called Banter House.

Her name was Skye, and Caleb had been coming to Banter House on Thursdays, the only day she worked. She was kind to everyone and had a smile that encouraged you to join her. With long brown hair and a friendly demeanor, she was the kind of woman his mother had told him to find and marry.

Those dreams were long gone. He wasn't the kind of man to marry. He definitely wasn't any woman's idea of good marriage material. He couldn't really explain why he had waited so long to deliver the package to her. When he first arrived, he found her working in the general store. She was a whirlwind, helping everyone.

That day had been a bad one for him. His leg had been a little stiff when he walked into the store.

He thought he had been tracking her, and then she had shown up with a chair. She smiled at him and told him to take a seat, that she'd be right with him. He sat down, and from then on, he couldn't just give her the package. Caleb couldn't remember the last time someone had looked out for him. At least he couldn't remember it happening and the person not being paid to do so.

"Skye, when you get a moment, can you help me?"

Skye. Her name was Skye. Caleb waited until her back was turned before he slipped out of the store. He would deliver his package. He just needed time. The package had waited a year. It could wait a few extra days.

He had been told he gave off an air of standoffishness. People and animals were wary around him. This slip of a girl had not only spoken to him, but she'd also managed to point out a weakness of his in public and offer to help him.

He watched her serve the crowd and decided he would deliver the package tomorrow. Tonight, he would watch the most beautiful and fearless woman he had ever met: Skye O'Malley.

I hope you enjoyed Hannah and Adam's story. Check out book 3 in the Love Happens series *Sweet Compromises* and read about Caleb and Skyes story.

Sign up to my newsletter to receive updates on new releases, sale promotions, and free books.

susanwarnerauthor.com